# ALIAS™
## DECLASSIFIED

# ALIAS™

## DECLASSIFIED

### THE OFFICIAL COMPANION

## MARK COTTA VAZ

BANTAM BOOKS

NEW YORK * TORONTO * LONDON * SYDNEY * AUCKLAND

ALIAS: DECLASSIFIED

A BANTAM BOOK / OCTOBER 2002

Text and cover art copyright © 2002 Touchstone Television
Unless otherwise credited, all photographs copyright © 2002 Touchstone Television

ISBN: 0-553-37597-0

Visit us on the Web! www.randomhouse.com

Published simultaneously in the United States and Canada

Bantam Books is an imprint of Random House Children's Books,
a division of Random House, Inc.
BANTAM BOOKS and the rooster colophon are registered trademarks of
Random House, Inc. Bantam Books,
1540 Broadway, New York, New York 10036

PRINTED IN THE UNITED STATES OF AMERICA

10 9 8 7 6 5 4 3 2 1

TO J. J. ABRAMS,
WHOSE GOOD HUMOR AND CREATIVE
SPIRIT ARE INFECTIOUS;

TO THE TALENTED CAST AND CREW,
WHO WELCOMED ME;

AND TO MY BELOVED SISTERS,
KATHERINE, MARIA, AND TERESA—
YOU GUYS ARE <u>SO</u> SYDNEY BRISTOW!

# ALIAS IS A STORY ABOUT IDENTITY.

A young woman loses her fiancé and learns her life is nothing like it seems. So begins a long, difficult, often painful search for the truth. Her relationships with her father and mother—a woman she once believed was dead—are beyond damaged. She must lie to her friends about her dangerous, secret life . . . all the while wishing she could be just one thing. Normal.

These are the elements that inspired the *Alias* series—along with the bonus opportunity to write about a beautiful, strong-willed, kick-ass action hero fighting her way to justice in exotic international locales.

But writing *Alias* is one thing. Producing it is another. Given the constraints of television, adapting our stories to film on a weekly basis is, let's just say, a challenge. Don't get me wrong: it's more fun than almost everything. But one thing it isn't is effortless.

When the idea of *Alias: Declassified* was pitched to me, I was thrilled. And not just because I kind of live for books like this (don't you love great behind-the-scenes books?). I was thrilled because *Alias* is blessed with the most stellar cast and crew ever assembled—an incredible group of people—and a volume like this would give readers a chance to meet some of them. Now, granted, I can't say enough good things about Jennifer Garner. Chances are she's nicer than you are. I mean seriously. And Victor Garber! Could he be better? No. What about Ron Rifkin? Or Carl? Or Michael or Merrin or Kevin or Bradley—all of them are just good, good, deeply good people who happen to be wonderful actors. But this book will introduce you to others who work equally hard. Perhaps harder. People whose names you most likely haven't heard before. They're geniuses, and I'm indebted to them all. They are the ones who make *Alias* possible.

The man who made this book possible is Mark Cotta Vaz. I'd like to thank Mark, a man we were obviously lucky to get (he's also the author of a number of those great books I'm talking about). Almost everyone Mark interviewed for this book later commented to me that it was a joy to have him around.

Finally, I'd like to state the obvious: We couldn't tell the story of Sydney Bristow without you. To those viewers who have watched rabidly from the beginning—and those who have only just caught their first episode— allow me, on behalf of everyone you're about to meet, to say thank you. We are more grateful than you know.

J. J. Abrams

# INTERNAL MEMORANDUM

FROM:       MARK COTTA VAZ

TO:         WENDY LOGGIA, EDITOR, RANDOM HOUSE

RE:         THEMES OF THE ALIAS: DECLASSIFIED PROJECT

When you first contacted me about my writing a book on the debut season of the *Alias* television series, the show's secret-agent scenario reminded me of the old *Mission: Impossible* series. Although no self-destructing tape was involved in my accepting this assignment—nor such potential perils as defusing nuclear devices with seconds ticking away—the notion of going behind the scenes to explore the making of an episodic spy thriller was as irresistible as any mission that'd stir the blood of the undercover crowd. I didn't have to scale walls or use deadly pressure-point kung-fu strikes to gain entry to *Alias*, either—I was happily given access during several trips to the production offices and sound-stages at the Walt Disney Studios lot in Burbank, California.

Before I flew to Burbank, I was drawn to a mythic font of the spy genre—some old, well-thumbed James Bond paperbacks. Unlike the suave movie incarnation, author Ian Fleming's agent 007 was a fatalistic Cold War warrior who believed he'd never live to enjoy a government pension. But what beguiled me was the author photo on a 1962 copy of *Doctor No*: Fleming casually holds a burning cigarette in his left hand, grips a black pistol in his right, and gazes with a Mona Lisa smile at some target beyond the borders of his portrait, implying that being a spy is a game, that potential death is the spice of espionage.

I don't know what Fleming would have made of *Alias* heroine Sydney Bristow, the secret agent played by Jennifer Garner. Women in Bond thrillers and the spy genre have usually been either bedroom trophies or beautiful seductresses. Sydney initially reminded me of an early exception, Diana Rigg's character, Emma Peel, from TV's classic *The Avengers*, but I ultimately realized that elegant Emma was merely another taste of eye candy. Sydney Bristow, however, is not only beautiful, but exceptionally brainy and very two-fisted—I think series creator J. J. Abrams broke the mold with this female secret agent.

*Alias* also poses manifold questions, is an enigma bound up with a weaving of narrative threads. An ongoing story line concerning fictitious Italian Renaissance scientist and seer Milo Rambaldi, whose manuscript and scattered artifacts are coveted by various global intelligence agencies, was an unfolding mystery throughout the first season, as was the earthshaking "Prophecy" mentioned in Rambaldi's deciphered codes. There was the secret espionage career of Jack Bristow, Sydney's estranged father. Her mother, Laura, lost in a river when Sydney's parents' car went off the road one fateful day, was only a childhood memory—and a ghost that would return to haunt both her and her father. As the season unfolded, it became clearer what ABC, the network that broadcasts the Touchstone television series, meant by the *Alias* promotional line "Sometimes the Truth Hurts."

On my first flight to Burbank on behalf of this project, I thought of how fact and folklore about governmental conspiracies and inscrutable prophecies form a background buzz, like scrambled static on TV in the dead of night when stations go off the air. That latter point was driven home the Sunday afternoon I checked into my hotel, located a short walk from the fabled Disney lot where each weekly episode of *Alias* is produced. John, a jovial desk clerk dressed in a blue suit and Mickey Mouse tie, served up an only-in-L.A. moment as he regaled me with—shades of the Rambaldi manuscript—an account of the deciphering of ancient Sumerian texts detailing helixes comprising the genetic code of Adam and Eve. "Without truth there can be no illusion," he added enigmatically.

The surreal fun continued as I switched on my hotel-room television to that night's *Alias* episode and realized how near I was to the gated dream factory where each installment was produced. "Q & A," that night's show, was the seventeenth episode of the twenty-two-show season and a look back, complete with expositive scenes from past episodes—a "clip show." Retold was college student Sydney Bristow's recruitment by SD-6, which she thought was a secret CIA division, and her subsequent shattering realization that SD-6 was evil, followed by her decision to become a double agent receiving countermissions from the CIA. Sydney's personal pain was again laid bare as she relived the revelation that her dead mother had been a KGB agent. The Rambaldi Prophecy, and the possibility of Sydney's being the fulfillment of that vision, brought things up to date. At the hour's end, our indomitable heroine, driving off on a mission to disprove the Prophecy, was pursued by police and drove her car off a pier—and experienced a chilling realization as she survived what should have been her watery grave.

The next morning, I was taken to the *Alias* production office by way of a zigzagging pedestrian bridge connecting the ABC building with the Disney lot. I quickly discovered that all my meditations on spy stuff and influences ripped from today's headlines had to go out the window. Sure, most of *Alias*'s cast and production principals are steeped in pop culture and Bond fantasies, and the series certainly serves up the requisite action and adventure. But, I discovered, the show's spy-genre aspect is just the straw that stirs the drink. *Alias* is exploring something deeper, a powerful theme that was always there, hiding in plain sight.

But maybe that's the true nature of *Alias*, the very title redolent of secrets and hidden agendas. Knowing that things are never what they seem is practically a necessity for maintaining the illusion of a successful television program: Actors assume the identities of fictional characters, everything from Sydney Bristow's Los Angeles residence to the SD-6 offices takes place on soundstage sets, and far-flung world capitals are computer-processed images or locations shot in Burbank (often a bit of both).

The major themes explored during my mission are detailed in the attached dossiers. The following report will *not* self-destruct.

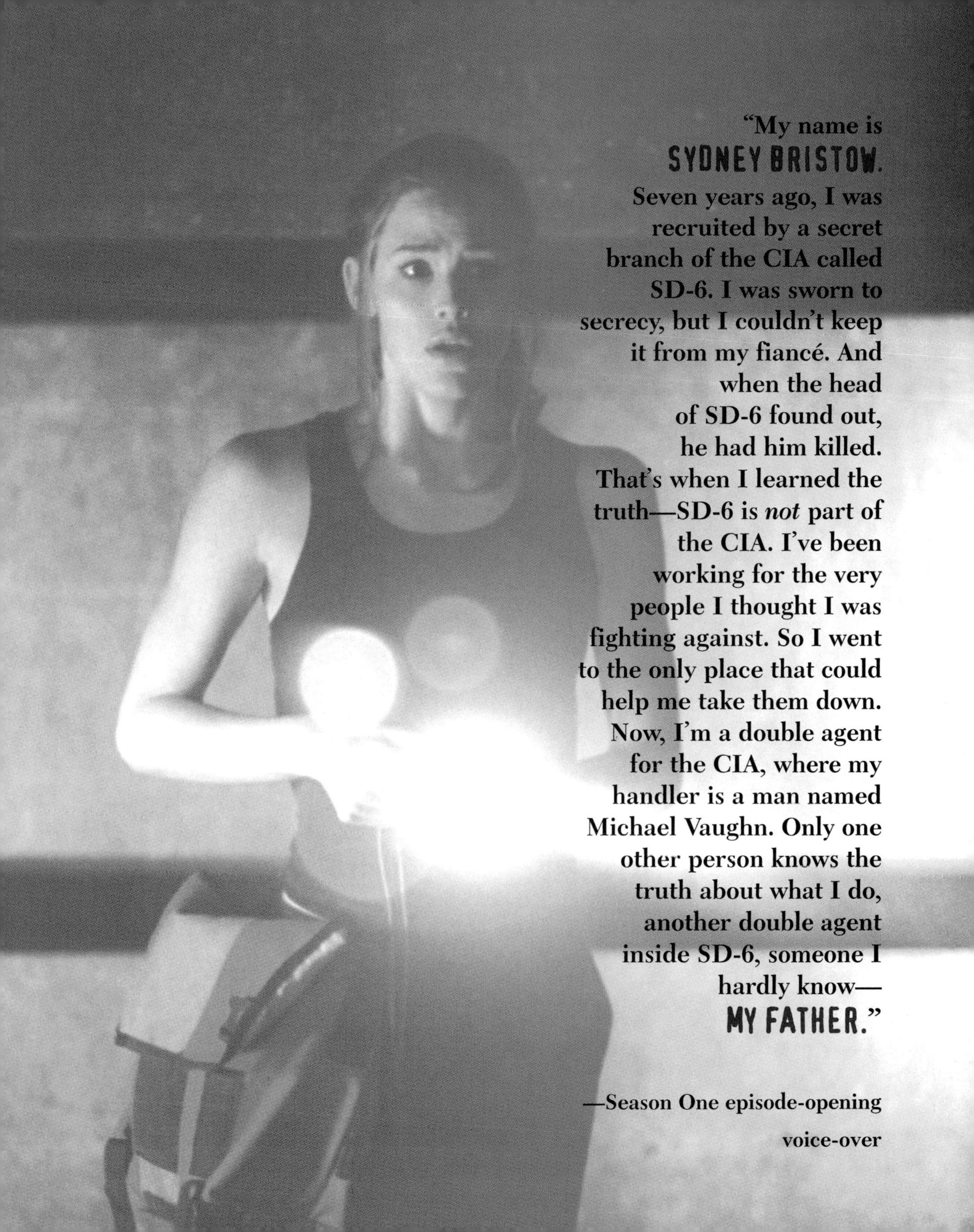

"My name is **SYDNEY BRISTOW**. Seven years ago, I was recruited by a secret branch of the CIA called SD-6. I was sworn to secrecy, but I couldn't keep it from my fiancé. And when the head of SD-6 found out, he had him killed. That's when I learned the truth—SD-6 is *not* part of the CIA. I've been working for the very people I thought I was fighting against. So I went to the only place that could help me take them down. Now, I'm a double agent for the CIA, where my handler is a man named Michael Vaughn. Only one other person knows the truth about what I do, another double agent inside SD-6, someone I hardly know— **MY FATHER**."

—Season One episode-opening

voice-over

# REPORT CONTENTS

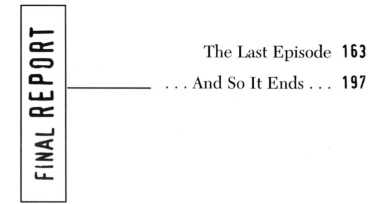

THE DOSSIERS

FINAL REPORT

# JENNIFER GARNER

was quietly building a résumé of roles in such films as *Deconstructing Harry* and *Pearl Harbor*, and had a recurring role in the TV series *Felicity* before being cast in the *Alias* starring role by series creator J. J. Abrams (who also co-created *Felicity*).

aka **SYDNEY BRISTOW**, a student at UCLA when she is recruited by SD-6. Working undercover as an employee for an SD-6 front, the Credit Dauphine bank in Los Angeles, Sydney breaks the ultimate SD-6 commandment by revealing her secret life to her fiancé, Danny Hecht. His ensuing murder and her realization that SD-6 is an enemy organization have given her a new purpose—to bring down SD-6 while operating as a double agent for the CIA.

# VICTOR GARBER

is a storied stage star who has received four Tony nominations. He is also a veteran television actor. Garber's film work includes roles in *Legally Blonde* and *Titanic*, in which he played the architect of the doomed luxury ship.

aka **JACK BRISTOW,** Sydney's long-estranged father, who also leads a life as a CIA double agent working undercover at SD-6. He bears the burden of knowing that his once beloved wife was KGB and married him to get CIA secrets.

## RON RIFKIN

was awarded a Tony in 1998 for Best Supporting Actor in *Cabaret*. His film work ranges from Woody Allen productions to *JFK*, *L.A. Confidential*, and *The Majestic*.

aka **ARVIN SLOANE**, the ruthless head of SD-6, who ordered the death of Sydney's fiancé and is a key player in the Alliance, an evil umbrella organization encompassing SD-6 and eleven other secret agencies. About his mysterious past, a few facts have surfaced: Sloane's espionage career began at the CIA, and he has known Sydney since she was a little girl.

## MICHAEL VARTAN,

born in Paris and raised in the village of Fleury, moved to Los Angeles when he was eighteen and took up acting. His career includes roles in such films as *The Pallbearer* (for which J. J. Abrams was a producer), *One Hour Photo*, and *Never Been Kissed*.

aka **AGENT MICHAEL VAUGHN**, a young, slightly green CIA operative and Sydney's handler at the agency. His affection for Sydney is the whispered talk around the agency water coolers.

# CARL LUMBLY,

a stage veteran who has appeared in such films as *Escape from Alcatraz, How Stella Got Her Groove Back,* and *Men of Honor,* has also had starring roles in the TV movie *Buffalo Soldiers* and the superhero television series *M.A.N.T.I.S.*

aka **AGENT MARCUS DIXON**, Sydney's regular partner on dangerous SD-6 missions. Dixon, along with nearly all his fellow operatives, mistakenly believes he's serving his country at SD-6.

# BRADLEY COOPER

graduated in 1997 from the honors English program at Georgetown University and moved to New York to pursue an acting career, relocating to L.A. when *Alias* beckoned.

aka **WILL TIPPIN**, a reporter for a major Los Angeles newspaper, who carries a torch for his unrequited love, Sydney Bristow. Tippin's reportorial instincts spur him to pursue the answers to lingering questions about Danny's murder, despite Sydney's objections and later without her knowledge. That path takes him into the deadly shadow world of espionage.

## KEVIN WEISMAN

is a founding member of the Buffalo Nights Theatre Company and has been featured in television (including *Felicity* and *The X-Files*) and movies (*Gone in Sixty Seconds*).

aka **MARSHALL**, high-tech nerd supreme of SD-6 and the go-to gadget and gizmo guy for equipping Sydney Bristow's missions.

## MERRIN DUNGEY

was a standout acting student at UCLA and from there developed *Black Like Who?*, a one-woman show for the HBO Comedy Workspace.

aka **FRANCIE CALFO**, who shares a house in Los Angeles with Sydney Bristow. She works as a party planner and knows *nothing* of Sydney's double life. Francie, unlucky in love, knows her friend will always be there for her—unless she's off on another one of those business trips for "the bank."

# ALIAS RECEIVED 11 EMMY NOMINATIONS FOR THE 2001-2002 SEASON:

## Outstanding Art Direction For A Single-Camera Series
*Alias*-Truth Be Told (Pilot)-ABC-Touchstone Television
Scott Chambliss, Production Designer; Cece Destefano, Art Director; Karen Manthey, Set Decorator

## Outstanding Casting for A Drama Series
*Alias*-ABC-Touchstone Television
Megan McConnell, C.S.A., Original Casting by; Janet Gilmore, C.S.A., Original Casting by;
April Webster, C.S.A., Casting by

## Outstanding Cinematography For A Single-Camera Series
*Alias*-Truth Be Told (Pilot)-ABC-Touchstone Television
Michael Bonvillain, Director of Photography

## Outstanding Costumes For A Series
*Alias*-Truth Be Told (Pilot)-ABC-Touchstone Television
Linda Serijan-Fasmer, Costume Designer; Anne Hartley, Costume Supervisor

## Outstanding Single-Camera Picture Editing For A Series
*Alias*-Q&A-ABC-Touchstone Television
Mary Jo Markey, Editor

## Outstanding Hairstyling For A Series
*Alias*-Q&A-ABC-Touchstone Television
Michael Reitz, Hairstylist; Karen Bartek, Hair Dresser

## Outstanding Makeup For A Series (Non-Prosthetic)
*Alias*-Q&A-ABC-Touchstone Television
Angela Nogaro, Makeup Artist; Diana Brown, Key Makeup Artist

## Outstanding Lead Actress In A Drama Series
*Alias*-ABC-Touchstone Television
Jennifer Garner as Sydney Bristow

## Outstanding Supporting Actor In A Drama Series
*Alias*-ABC-Touchstone Television
Victor Garber as CIA Agent Jack D. Bristow

## Outstanding Stunt Coordination
*Alias*-Q&A-ABC-Touchstone Television
Jeff Habberstad, Stunt Coordinator

## Outstanding Writing For A Drama Series
*Alias*-Truth Be Told (Pilot)-ABC-Touchstone Television
J.J. Abrams, Writer

. . . AND SO IT BEGINS . . .

It was a tight squeeze through a darkened corridor jammed with high-tech equipment. A bouncing penlight beam led the way into a dark and deserted main office that was empty except for scattered chairs and a few bare desks. The beam of light traced the open door of an inner office that, unlike the outer area, was furnished with an official-looking desk flanked by U.S. and CIA flags, the back wall emblazoned with the CIA shield.

"This space changes for both Agent Vaughn's and [CIA bureau chief] Devlin's offices and also serves as the office for the newspaper editor," Sean Gerace, an *Alias* writer's assistant, said of the inner office. "When it's the editor's office they put up wonderful old pictures of newspaper presses."

© 2002 SCOTT CHAMBLISS

**Welcome to SD-6.** The hallway from the SD-6 scanning room into the main office. The SD-6 office, along with Sydney Bristow's home and the CIA/newspaper offices, is part of the permanent set created by production designer Scott Chambliss's department and erected on Disney Studios' Stage 3 the first season.

SD-6, main office area. Operating on a budget in its first season, the production's challenge was to make more with less. Chambliss's design and DP Michael Bonvillain's photography combined to make SD-6 look huge, with a seemingly endless supply of agents on duty. (Note, in back, the glass doors to Arvin Sloane's office.)

With a ceiling in place, and without stage lights, the enclosed *Alias* set was gloomy, and the penlight beam gave this stop on the soundstage tour the feel of a break-in. The *Alias* cast and crew were away on a location shoot, and the outer office was in transition. When needed, that space could be dressed as the bustling newsroom where Will Tippin works or the corridors of power of the CIA's L.A. bureau.

Gerace led the way back out past the equipment jammed in the back corridor. The high-tech stuff normally dressed the office of SD-6 gadget wizard Marshall, he explained, but it had been moved here while that space was being transformed into something else.

Outside the double-duty set, hanging from the ceiling of a vast soundstage were two translights—gigantic screens printed with photographic city scenes—that could be lowered to create the illusion of a real world outside the office windows. The self-contained CIA/newsroom set was like a little box in a larger magic box, the enclosing space of the Walt Disney Studios' warehouse-sized Stage 3. The entire soundstage was deserted and eerily quiet, like a ghost town, but scattered around were the iconic landmarks that formed double agent Sydney Bristow's world in the show's first season.

**Arvin Sloane's inner sanctum.**

A few steps from the CIA/newsroom set was the house where Sydney and Francie lived. Here one could walk through a proper front door and into a place built without removable, or "floating," walls, an inviting place that allowed for a 360-degree camera view. Here was the decorated living room and kitchen space where Sydney and Francie and Will talked and laughed and hung out. There was Sydney's bedroom; by her bedside was a copy of Emily Brontë's *Wuthering Heights*, a book one might expect to find on the night table of a graduate student in literature. The intimate house had a bathroom, featuring the tub where Sydney often soaked to unwind after another death-defying mission.

Right around the corner was the dark side of Sydney's world—the SD-6 offices. These offices were different from those in the pilot that aired September 30, 2001. For the first show, SD-6 office scenes had been shot in a building in downtown L.A. For the season's official run, SD-6 was designed and built to include an entry scanning room and a long hallway to the main area. "The location space they used for the pilot was dark and concrete. They were limited by that building," Gerace explained. "But the art department did an incredible job creating an ultratech environment. It would have been cost prohibitive to build sets for a one-time deal, but when the show was picked up, they took a little liberty when building these sets, so SD-6 changed from the pilot."

**Welcome to Sydney's house! The front door opens onto a scene Scott Chambliss describes as a "warm, young, and contemporary Los Angeles feeling." The missing roof, however, reveals that "home" is a soundstage set.**

The main SD-6 work area had an industrial-tech feeling. The set was without a ceiling, allowing for lowering and raising lights, with sliding walls to move equipment in and out and provide entrances and exits for characters. Sturdy-looking columns were actually plastered plywood, with high-tech looking (but nonfunctioning) cables attached to each agent's desk. "There are only some twenty desks here," noted Gerace, "but when it's lit and they smoke it up to get that texture for film, it's amazing. The way they shoot, it seems like endless agents. They always try to make the space seem bigger than it is."

The living room area in Sydney's home.

Off the main area was the conference room where Sydney, Dixon, Marshall, Jack Bristow, and SD-6 leader Arvin Sloane regularly discussed their missions. Sloane's office was adjacent, his black chair seemingly radiating the character's menacing energy—strangely, the visitors kept their distance from Sloane's seat of power.

As Sean Gerace led the way out into the sunshine of the Disney lot, he recalled how the CIA bureau-office lobby seen in the pilot was staged downtown at the Los Angeles Center Studios. "When we were shooting at L.A. Studios, the movies *Planet of the Apes* and Kevin Spacey's *K-Pax* were also being filmed there." Gerace smiled. "We'd have our radios and there'd be a little cross-chatter: 'Gorillas, go over to Stage Two.' Once, we left our CIA offices after shooting all night and headed down to the lobby, where we got lost—and ended up in the middle of a mental institution! It was the *K-Pax* set. It was quite surreal."

On the set with Victor Garber, Jennifer Garner, and J. J. Abrams.

# INNER SANCTUM

The Disney Feature Animation Building in Burbank is like a cartoon come to life, a structure festooned with a purple tower based on Mickey Mouse's peaked wizard's cap from the "Sorcerer's Apprentice" segment of *Fantasia,* while a roof in the shape of a ship's prow recalls the Mad Hatter's hat from Disney's animated *Alice in Wonderland.* Across the courtyard is the ABC building. The Disney company acquired the ABC network in 1995, the year the Animation Building was completed. The two companies are historically connected—ABC was a partner in Disneyland and aired such classic Disney TV shows as *The Mickey Mouse Club*—and that link today is literal, with another cartoon-like icon, a zigzagging pedestrian bridge, reaching from the ABC towers to the walled domain of the Disney lot.

Even while working together at SD-6, father and daughter keep their distance. The show itself is its own alias—the saga of a dysfunctional family.

Just off the bridge, on the edge of the studio grounds, are the glass-walled *Alias* production offices, the nerve center where the twenty-two-episode first season was plotted and the production planned. The atmosphere was almost college dorm–like, with the unpretentious space unadorned by fancy furniture, the staff dressed in Southern California casual, and the area outside creator J. J. Abrams's office crowded with Ping-Pong and foosball tables.

The game room tables had no players. "Q & A," the seventeenth episode,

**Pictured left to right, executive producer and regular series director Ken Olin, Jennifer Garner, and camera operator Ross Judd view the playback of a shot. On the set, Olin likes to put the creative energy of cast and crew into actual filming and not spend too much time rehearsing, a sentiment shared by star Garner. "Jennifer likes to work fast, and that's helped sustain the pace of the series," Olin notes.**

had aired the previous night, and with five episodes left in the season, production principals were behind closed doors, crafting the last chapters that would culminate in the final episode. Jesse Alexander, one of the show's writers, appeared, shaking his head at the awful realization that the cushion of time they'd enjoyed early in the season was over.

"Production is like a freight train, and the writers are running on the track ahead of the train," explained John Eisendrath, who, along with Abrams and Ken Olin, was a series executive producer. "In the beginning of the year you're way in front of the train. It's like, 'Where's the train, I don't see the train?' But, by episode sixteen the train is right behind you."

But time was never a luxury anyway, considering the show's ambitions. J. J. Abrams himself explained that the pilot, which he scripted and directed, had been a seemingly impossible mission. There'd been only ten weeks for scripting, casting, and production prep, and only twenty days to shoot the movie-length pilot (with its two-hour airtime). All the while hanging in the creative balance was the network's decision on whether to order a full season of episodes.

"It was impossible!" Abrams exclaimed. "This wasn't like casting a play or a movie. If it worked—and that was the hope—the show could be running for years. So we were casting people who not only had to look good and be right for their parts, they had to work well together. That was important, because our show is a semi-ensemble, with players not existing out of context but constantly referencing each other. It had to be a collaborative, communal effort."

**Jim Jost, 2nd assistant camera, and director of photography Michael Bonvillain.**

# ORIGIN STORY

*Alias*'s Sarah Caplan—the line producer and "field general" who oversaw production logistics and ensured that each episode met its budget—was working with Abrams during the pilot. When they won a series run, she saw to "the blueprint," as she called it, for the season's budget and costs per episode. "I feel like we make a little movie every week," Caplan said. "The pilot was very ambitious, and we continued to maintain that level of ambition throughout the season."

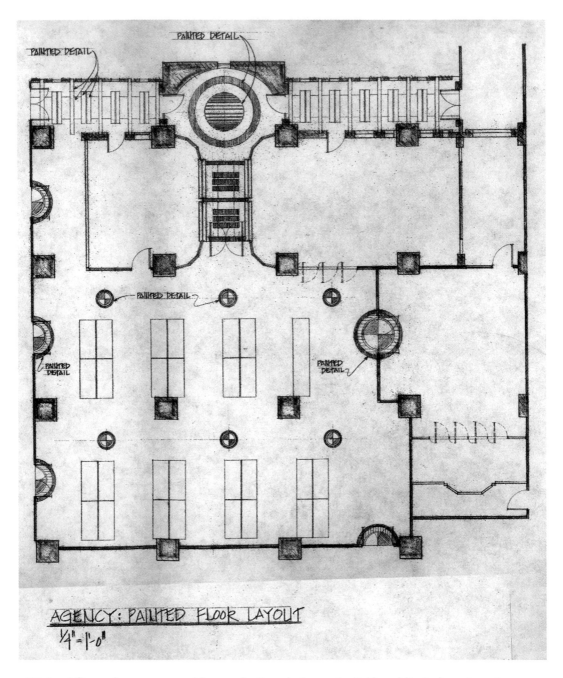

PAINTED DETAIL

PAINTED DETAIL

PAINTED DETAIL

PAINTED DETAIL

PAINTED DETAIL

PAINTED DETAIL

AGENCY: PAINTED FLOOR LAYOUT
$\frac{1}{4}'' = 1'-0''$

SD-6 set floor plans, prepared by production designer Scott Chambliss's department.

Despite the frenetic schedule for episodic TV, the show was infused with feature-film production values from the start. That Abrams brought a features aesthetic to *Alias* wasn't an accident. His love of movies went back, he recalled, to when he was eight and a grandfather treated him to the Universal Studios tour. That night he began lobbying to borrow his dad's Super 8 film camera. After several refusals, his father, a successful television producer, relented. Many years and amateur films later, Abrams was writing screenplays for such films as *Armageddon*, and his production credits ranged from the feature *Forever Young* to the *Felicity* TV series.

Abrams, like many young filmmakers who grew up with movies and videos and comic books, has memory circuits wired to the mythic mainframe of pop culture. As one of the new generation of creators, he dreams of paying homage to those classic archetypes but also wants to craft new myths. "What I love about *Alias*, and in a weird way the point of it, is I wanted to create something that was an amalgam of everything I love, something that had action and special effects and was funny and depressing and emotional. A few years ago somebody asked me what type of movie I'd like to do first and I said *American Werewolf in London*. It wasn't an important movie, but it was *so* entertaining. It was a B genre done A.

"I had this deal with [Disney] Touchstone to develop a show and I didn't want to do something that felt like everything else on network TV. I wanted to do a television series closer to that spirit of *American Werewolf in London*, a familiar genre done with intelligence. TV doesn't typically do that kind of thing. It does medical shows really well, it's great with police and courtroom dramas. But you have to look to Fox and the WBs of the world to find more fringe, out-there stuff."

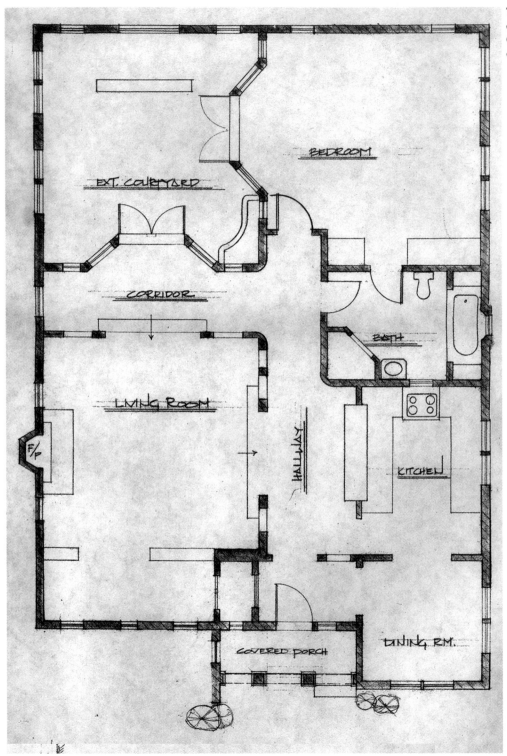

BEDROOM

EXT. COURTYARD

CORRIDOR

BATH

LIVING ROOM

HALLWAY

F/P

KITCHEN

COVERED PORCH

DINING RM.

Abrams had been fascinated with the idea of characters with a double life and was developing a story line about a young boy with a secret side, an idea he shelved when *Harry Potter* appeared. He'd also loved James Bond movies and had dreamed up spy stories back in elementary school. Those two fascinations—characters with a double life and the thrills of espionage—came together in the writers' room of *Felicity*. It was during a brainstorming session in that show's third season that Abrams proposed a wild scenario: "I said, 'Wouldn't it be incredibly cool if Felicity were recruited by the CIA, because she could go on incredible missions and have kick-ass fights and stunts!' I said it as a joke, because *Felicity* is about sweet, romantic people in college and it's a hard show to come up with stories for.

"But I wrote down these ideas about a grad school student who lived a double life and had trouble with Dad. I kept thinking about these characters and what their secrets and emotional lives would be. Any story about a family where there are secrets, and what happens when those truths emerge, was fascinating to me. I started to get excited by that and pitched it to Touchstone at the end of 2000."

And that's one of the hidden truths of *Alias*, the percolating theme that came to a boil in Abrams's mind: For all its spy-genre trappings, the show at its heart is about a dysfunctional family. "On the face of it, the idea of a spy who goes to grad school is ludicrous," Abrams chuckled. "But what interested me is this vulnerable woman who's on the brink of having the closest thing to a normal life she's ever had. And she tells her fiancé the truth and it's all destroyed. Her life is turned upside down and she realizes who she's really working for and who her father really is. It's a spy show, but at its core is the relationship between this young woman and her father. I got excited about what happens to her, what that person would be like."

Key to bringing that woman to life was Abrams's casting of the little-known Jennifer Garner as Sydney Bristow. There were some doubts at the outset, but Touchstone and ABC "didn't put up a fight about her," Abrams said. In retrospect, it was one of those casting calls that are the stuff of Hollywood legend. "Jennifer has so exceeded everyone's expectations," Abrams enthused. "She's clearly beautiful, she's smart and funny. But I also saw something wild under the surface—she reminded me of Clark Kent. You don't want to look at somebody and go, Damn, she can kick ass! She has this quality of the girl next door, the girl you'd want to know or date or be. And then the surprise—she's lethal."

# INTO THE FOG

Unlike programs that have a "series bible," detailing every aspect of series mythology, *Alias* was the stuff of dreams and brainstorms. There were, of course, a structure and a grand design. But generally, everyone from creator and cast to production heads and crew was all on a creative caravan, literally making things up as they journeyed into a creative landscape of often murky, cloudy terrain.

"It's funny, because the pilot felt like driving in the fog," Abrams concluded. "We were starting up the car and in the distance you could see, barely, the shape of this mountain you're going to be heading towards. The whole season was driving through this fog where, as you went along, you started seeing details you couldn't see at first. And we couldn't anticipate all the turns we had to make to reach that mountain."

THE WRITERS' ROOM

In this drawing, pinned to the writers' room bulletin board the first season, creator J. J. Abrams is pictured dreaming up the world of *Alias*. Executive producer John Eisendrath explains the writing staff's job is to "help figure out this world [J.J.] created. . . ."

# BULLETIN BOARD

The buzz about *Alias* began in earnest when Jennifer Garner won a Golden Globe for Best Actress for her role as double agent Sydney Bristow. An ensuing *Time* magazine feature article (February 4, 2002) wryly noted how incongruous it was for such an honor to go to someone in what was, on the surface, an action-hero role: "Best-actress laurels don't normally go to ladies who lunge. . . ."

In the following months, Garner became a familiar face on the cover of magazines from *Rolling Stone* to *Entertainment Weekly*. The *EW* article (March 8, 2002) recounted Garner's own real-life spy move, the time she'd gone to the *Alias* production offices looking for J. J. Abrams and noticed the open door to the writers' room. She stealthily entered and viewed a bulletin board crowded with index cards detailing the key beats for characters and plot points. She scanned every card and slipped out ahead of footsteps coming from down the hall. "I was so excited about pulling a spy move that I forgot everything that I'd read," she sighed to writer Dan Snierson. "If I could just find out what this last *moment* of the year is that J.J. keeps talking about, *that* would be the greatest mission of my life."

Less harried visitors to the writers' room—the writers themselves—spent countless hours here. A first-season visit revealed a relatively spartan place with a long table surrounded by chairs, an adjoining kitchen, and windows providing a welcome view of the outdoors. Despite the presence of a punching bag sculpted to resemble the face and torso of a generic cartoon man (a gift from writer Jesse Alexander), the infamous bulletin board dominated the room. Testament to the storytelling ambitions of *Alias*, the bulletin board was covered with dozens of color-coded

The villains of *Alias* posed a challenge for the writers the first season. "Sloane is a villain, but Sydney is already undercover, working against him," explains writer Jesse Alexander. "We didn't need a villain of the week, but someone about every three episodes Sydney could focus on and bring down so we understand that she's being successful."

"At the start we didn't want to be like a comic book—Mr. Freeze is back!" adds writer Roberto Orci. "Now we want recurring villains." Some of the most infamous appear on these pages.

"Suit and Glasses" was the only scripted description for the Taiwanese torturer (played by Ric Young) who practiced his unique form of dentistry in the pilot and final first-season episode.

cards tacked in rows marking each episode, detailing shorthand plot points and missions for each character.

Also pinned to the board was a drawing of J. J. Abrams with a thought balloon hanging over his head like a storm cloud, filled with caricatures of his *Alias* characters. Abrams is the creative font, but when a production is conjuring a mythology, the mythmaking, by necessity, is collaborative.

"A TV series is too big for any one person to come up with all of the ideas," John Eisendrath explained. "J.J. is incredibly gifted, but very gen-

**Ex-SD-6 agent and certifiable sadist McKenas Cole (Quentin Tarantino) taunts a captured Jack Bristow during his daring takeover of SD-6 on behalf of the mystery figure The Man.**

erous in acknowledging and accepting ideas. My main job is organizing the writing staff and getting the writing far enough along so J.J. can be looking after the rest of the show. It's a collective undertaking and a skill to figure out this world he created, to figure out what's in his head. That's the nature of the beast."

**Edward Poole, Machiavellian head of the British SD-9 arm of the Alliance (played to perfection by former *Saint* and James Bond star Roger Moore).**

# THE FIFTH ACT

In the writers' room a core eight-person team would brainstorm ideas for each episode for about a week and a half, helped along by Abrams, Eisendrath, and technical consultant Rick Orci (brother of Roberto, one of the writers). When each episode's story structure was "broken," a member of the team would write an outline (the writers took turns on a revolving basis), and a script draft was delivered ideally within a week or two to J. J. Abrams's office. Abrams and his staff worked the draft to completion, garnering feedback from production departments on the feasibility of the scripted locations, stunts, and effects.

*Alias* storytelling, however, was complicated by what Eisendrath called "the fifth-act motif," a style bound up in the show's decision to revive the classic cliffhanger that was

The imperious Arvin Sloane is bound and tortured in the episode "The Box." The predicaments and plot twists hatched in the writers' room for all the characters were a continual source of surprise for the actors. "We [the actors] are not part of the actual writing process; they lock themselves in their room. I once snuck into the writers' room—the door was open, no one was around," Ron Rifkin confides. "There was a huge bulletin board with every character's throughline. I got really nervous—I didn't want to find out anything. I quickly left!"

Abrams calls the show's writers "the living bible" of the series' evolving mythology. "We talk about things forward and backwards, up and down, in three dimensions." Abrams smiles. "Ultimately, to get to the deeper levels of plot twists and revelations, the audience makes the same journey as we do." Once each script is completed, the production generally has some eight days to shoot the episode. Here are writers Jeff Pinkner, Alex Kurtzman, Rudy Gaborno, Erica Messer, Debra Fisher, Crystal Nix Hines, Jesse Alexander, and Rick Orci.

once a staple of movie serials, as he explained: "In the typical four-act show, an episode opens with a one- or two-minute teaser, goes right to a commercial, and the end of the third act is when the character is in greatest peril. But, from the beginning, we discussed having our episodes end as often as possible with Sydney in jeopardy and the next episode opening with her figuring out how to extricate herself. So our show usually opens with a resolution of the previous episode's cliffhanger—and goes on for eight or ten minutes before the first commercial. We essentially decided to go with five acts."

Writer Jesse Alexander smiled as he recalled how the cliffhanger style was inspired by a strange phenomenon Abrams noted on *Felicity*, his first TV series: The show got its biggest ratings whenever a season ended on a cliffhanger. "So J.J. was like, 'Screw it, I want one of those every episode! I want people to watch!' So that's what brought about this cliffhanger structure we're devoted to."

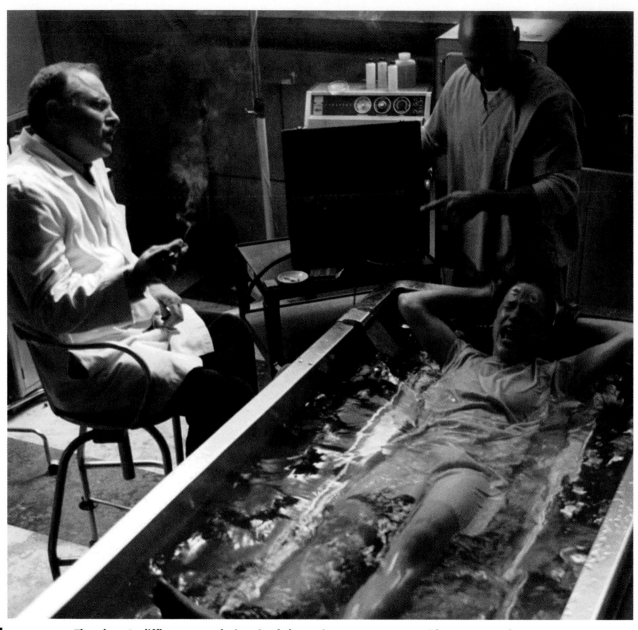

The show's cliffhanger style inspired the writers to come up with some novel torture scenes to test Sydney, such as this electroshock bath administered under the watchful eye of K-Directorate villain Kreshnik (Eugene Lazarev).

"There's a definite feeling on the set when there's [a torture scene] going on," Jennifer Garner says. "It's hard, because you have to go there mentally, and that's exhausting. But you have to have an imagination. It's like any acting job. It's just that mine makes me imagine crazier things than normal."

Alexander and Abrams met during their days at Sarah Lawrence College in Bronxville, New York, and teamed up to write a maiden script Alexander recalled as "like *Goonies* with machine guns." That script went nowhere, but better things were ahead for both of them. Alexander is now part of the *Alias* writing staff and has made his first script sale (the summer 2002 Warner Brothers release *Eight Legged Freaks*, a sci-fi monster movie).

"I have an affinity for action and spy stuff, but the biggest challenge for me was getting a handle on the expository nature of television writing, to make that feel natural," Alexander reflected. "It's an incredible art to make all the events seem like a seamless part of the lives of the characters. And with the serialized, cliffhanger structure of our show, none of our episodes are 'stand-alones,' each is like part of one epic tale. There's so much that has to be imparted about Sydney's mom and dad and fiancé and SD-6 and this Rambaldi guy and the CIA— it's just crazy! It's a challenge getting everybody on the same page, but it's an amazing process when it works well. Someone spins an idea that sets everybody else off."

## TENT POLES

At the beginning of the season, writers'-room sessions laid the groundwork for the episode-by-episode plotting ahead, outlining everything from potential SD-6 missions to character relationships. An overall plan was hammered out during this seminal stage, with plot points and revelations planned for specific episodes—guideposts visible through the fog-shrouded season ahead.

"A tent pole was Sydney finding out her mother was a KGB agent by the middle of the season," Alexander explained. "What precluded us from having a lot of major beats worked out from the start was J.J. likes to stay light on his feet and be able to change things right up to the last minute. We've had production people ask to look at the *Alias* bible—there is no *Alias* bible. Shows like *Star Trek* have massive guides, but we just have the scripts and the episodes themselves."

But the narrative "tent poles" were of sturdy construction. Roberto Orci noted that "from day one" they wanted the season to end with Sydney's mom returning from the dead, "popping out in some crazy way," as the head of an evil espionage organization. Another early idea was that Sydney would find herself in the same deadly situation her mother had faced, trapped in a sunken car and facing a watery death. In the resulting episode, "Q & A," Sydney escaped by sucking oxygen from the tire valve. "That's one of the things I pushed for at the beginning," Orci explained, "that Sydney find herself in the same scenario her mother was in when she supposedly died. So if Sydney can survive, she realizes perhaps her mother survived the same situation. That was a big tent pole we worked on in the early days."

## STORY STRUGGLES

The writers' room can be a creative battleground, and the writers have their war stories. "I'd have liked to have seen Will framed for the death of Danny," Orci smiled. "As a reporter, he's getting too close to SD-6, so they plant the gun that killed Sydney's fiancé in his car and suddenly he's on trial! After all, he's in love with Sydney, so he could be suspected of having killed Danny in a jealous rage. But nobody went for that, I was a lone voice on that one."

Some ideas instantly resonated. There was complete agreement on the idea that Sydney accidentally meet Danny's killer, a brainwashed and programmed SD-6 assassin whose lost memory of the killing is, sadly and ironically, brought to the surface by Sydney herself (presented in episode 7, "Color-Blind").

**Francie and Charlie gamble on their relationship during an ill-fated Vegas trip. Their failed love affair—once imagined as leading to a season-ending wedding—was a casualty of the writers' room.**

# THE LIFE AND DEATH OF CHARACTERS

In episodic TV main characters evolve, minor figures become major ones, and some characters come from nowhere. "And sometimes, when there's nothing left, a character has to die," added Orci. One such character was Charlie, Francie's fiancé (played by Evan Dexter Parke). The "exit strategy," as Orci put it, was to write Charlie as cheating on Francie, leading to a big breakup. Good-bye, Charlie!

Sydney's domestic world and spy life meet as she greets her secret SD-6 partner, Dixon, at the door of a Halloween party she's hosting at home. "Sydney juggles these dual lives," writer Alexander notes. "We always have to figure how to insert her home life in a way that feels as important dramatically as her spy world. But if her roommate is dealing with a cheating boyfriend and Sydney has to go shut off a nuclear bomb, it's a tough balancing act!"

"The potential was we'd follow his music career, play out his engagement with Francie," Orci explained. "The problem was the story line of Francie and Charlie wasn't working because you needed to see them together and that tended to isolate them from the rest of the story. It was important to have a family dynamic between Sydney, Will, and Francie—Charlie was getting in the way of the symmetry of that. We had to save one of them, so we chose to save Francie."

Curiously, one of the toughest of the regular characters to write was actor Bradley Cooper's Will Tippin, the crusading young reporter whose love for Sydney leads him to pursue the unexplained murder of her fiancé. The *Alias* production, which had monitored public reaction to the show through focus groups and Internet message boards, discovered, to their astonishment, that many fans hated Will.

"At least towards the end of the season we didn't have that vehemence we had at the beginning—'just kill him and get it over with!' " Alexander sighed. "That was incredible for us, because the staff *loves* him. He's a great actor, he's fun, he brings a great side to the show. It might just have been that viewers were protective of Sydney. After all, Sydney had asked him to stop investigating Danny's death, so he was acting in opposition to our main character. But Will cares about Sydney, he was doing things for the right reasons. But how to tell the best version of that story, how to properly serve the Will character, was the most intense thing we had to deal with all year."

That fan reaction, Cooper admitted, was "a total shock," and he initially wondered if he might be playing the character wrong. He huddled with J. J. Abrams, and their conclusion was that the audience, knowing things the character didn't know, were two steps ahead of Will, grimly anticipating the damage his actions could cause. "It was always clear to me that

Will was trying to protect Sydney—he had no idea she's a secret agent," Cooper sighed. "For some reason, the audience didn't make that leap to get into his shoes, to see that point of view. So that was a tough road for me. But that's what I love about Will [that he doesn't easily back down]. I hope that he's sort of an Everyman taking audiences into these outlandish circumstances, that Will is almost the eyes for the viewer."

Some new characters were strokes of luck—or creative desperation. In a serendipitous moment, Alexander was at a Hanukkah party and saw an actor friend, Joey Slotnick, who seemed perfect for a role Alexander was scripting for "The Box," a two-part episode. Alexander invited the actor, with Abrams's blessing, to come aboard as CIA agent Haladki, a by-the-book stickler adept at backstabbing office politics who blows the whistle on Agent Vaughn for having purchased a Christmas gift for Sydney. "To see this great actor, who was perfect for this part, at this party was like, 'Oh, my God, we're so screwed—*save us!*'" Alexander laughed. "And Joey was so good that we realized the Haladki character opened our world and gave us so many more story possibilities."

"The Haladki character is a perfect example of how J.J. has a basic framework but can go with the flow," observed Michael Vartan. "The part was originally planned for that one episode, but Joey was so great, and we all loved him so much, that J.J. said, 'Hey! Screw this—he's going to be in more!' The cool thing about J.J. is he gets all these crazy ideas at the last minute and we get rewrites at the last minute, but it's definitely worth it in the long run. His mind is a *really* active place!"

"The Box" had originally been planned as a single episode but was expanded into a two-parter on the urging of producer Sarah Caplan, who noticed the script had a staggering 190 scenes and pointed out that it would be technically impossible to get everything into one hour's air-

**Sydney and a former lover, SD-6 agent Noah Hicks (Peter Berg), pose as hikers to infiltrate an underground complex that contains a computer with information about Alexander Khasinau, believed to be The Man. When this storyline was developing, the writers' room code name for Sydney's former flame was Zorro.**

time. The episode had been expanding, in part, as the writers indulged their vision for a role John Eisendrath characterized as initially being "the generic bad guy who wreaked havoc" during a daring takeover of SD-6 on behalf of The Man, a mysterious figure who wants a Rambaldi artifact that's in the SD-6 vaults. When famed filmmaker Quentin Tarantino was cast as that bad guy, ex-SD-6 agent McKenas Cole, the writers knew they had the potential for crafting a memorable villain.

"When we found out Tarantino had the part, we pulled this all-nighter in the writers' room to write this new character, sort of 'Tarantinoed' the script," said Alexander, who scripted with Eisendrath. "Quentin has a specific way of acting, his characters include pop references and speak with an almost musical rhythm, so we wrote the part specifically for him. He liked what we did and was really into it."

For Cole, the break-in would also be payback as he tortures Sloane with venom-tipped "needles of fire" (but fails to break the stoic SD-6 leader). "Once we knew it was Tarantino, a back story emerged of his relationship with SD-6, that he even had a crush on Sydney from when he first saw her at SD-6," Eisendrath added. "We also played out a disgruntled attitude he has for Arvin Sloane, selling that with a back story about Cole having been on an SD-6 mission and left for dead. The final script reflected a larger-than-life persona for that character, which hadn't been there before Quentin was cast."

"Another thing about 'The Box' was Cole is opening the SD-6 safe to get a box that's a Rambaldi artifact—and we didn't know what that was going to be," Alexander added. "One idea was that it was a special Rambaldi signet ring, then it was, 'How about a jar of clear liquid, something that could be anything we wanted it to be?' So that liquid ended up being used as the wash used on a recovered page of the Rambaldi manuscript to make this hidden image of Sydney Bristow appear [episode 15, "Page 47"]! We hadn't originally planned on that, but it felt organic, this notion that the Rambaldi book was written in a secret ink that's revealed when you apply the liquid from this vial."

The cast assembled. "What's cool about television is you live with the characters longer than in a movie story," says writer Orci. "From episode to episode they begin to define themselves on screen. Our show is like an action soap opera. You have to keep track of a lot of characters."

"It's such an eclectic group, and a real blessing how close we've all gotten," Bradley Cooper says of his co-stars. "The more at ease you are as people and friends, the easier it is to enter into this imaginary world together."

Roberto Orci noted that a good show is more than what's on the surface—it's about the underlying and guiding metaphor. "For example, *Buffy* is a metaphor for teen angst; jocks turning into werewolves is how we thought of people in high school who stuffed you in lockers." He smiled. "What you want to have in your mind [as a writer] is you're telling a metaphor. One of the organizing principles of *Alias* is it's about a screwed-up family who happen to be spies. That's the disguise—this is about a dysfunctional family."

There were some changes in the aftermath of the synchronized terrorist attacks on America on September 11, 2001, a day on which the *Alias* writers were in the creative terrain between episodes 5 and 6. One change was the World Trade Organization, slated to be a terrorist target in episode 4. Instead, it became the fictitious United Commerce Organization (UCO) when "A Broken Heart" aired on October 21, 2001. Sydney was also scripted to mention patriotism as a motivation for becoming a secret agent, there was continued emphasis on the CIA as "white hats" who follow the rules, and there were a few references to the actual USA PATRIOT Act passed in the wake of the attacks.

But other than those cosmetic textures, the world of *Alias* by season's end remained, as in the pilot, an escapist one. "We rarely do ripped-from-the-headlines stories," Eisendrath explained. "It's less creative to be topical, it's harder to create a world that's truly original. Elements of this world are cutting edge and real, but the world itself is fantastic. So we're unaffected by the headlines. We just follow the characters to wherever it is they're going."

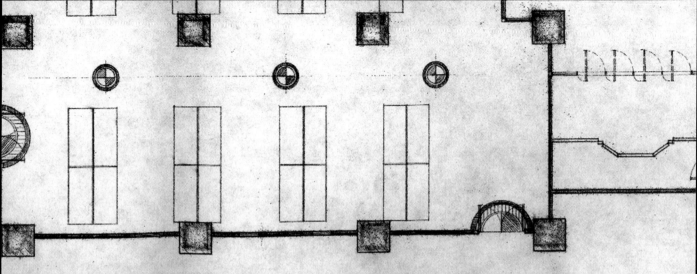

AGENCY: PAINTED FLOOR LAYOUT

¼" = 1'-0"

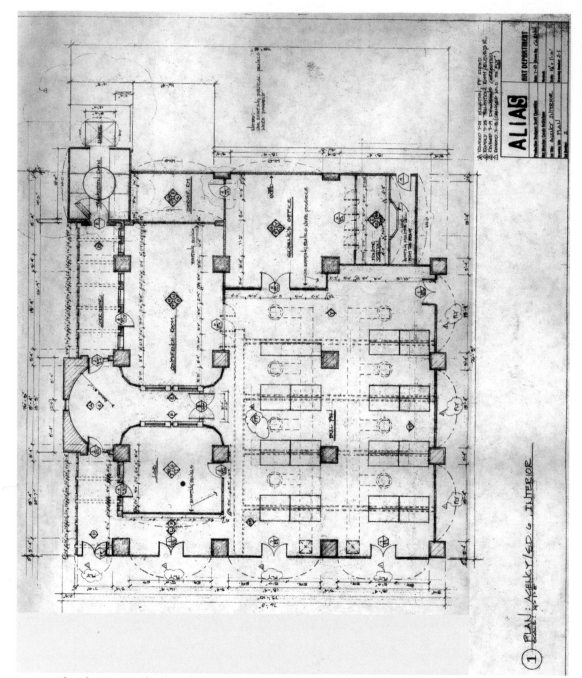

The show's production design department had to work up blueprints for the permanent sets—such as this SD-6 floor plan. (Hmmm. Did McKenas Cole get his hands on this floor plan before he broke into SD-6?)

# DREAMING UP THE WORLD

Among the core *Alias* team from the beginning was director of photography Michael Bonvillain, who recalled how the foundation for the world was carefully laid out in the pilot. "We didn't want to do something super comic-booky, but we didn't want to be super realistic, either. The look itself is a heightened realism with a lot of camera movement and color and contrast, a look that also gives viewers the feeling they're traveling to a variety of places each episode."

The art of cinematography involves more than having the director of photography (or DP) aim a camera and shoot—there's shot composition and setting up the lights. The color palette is also key, although an early production decision to have a special color for each episode (such as restricting the use of red to specifics like Sydney's wig in the pilot) was abandoned as the season wore on. However, a guiding color scheme, and even certain camera movements, remained a vital production value. "Sydney's personal life was designed to have a warmer look, and those shots use longer lenses and the camera movement isn't as frenetic," Bonvillain explained. "In contrast with her home life, there's a lot more chaos and camera motion when we enter SD-6, along with a desaturated, blue-gray look. We also smoke the main agents' area of SD-6 because it lowers contrast and makes for a subtle aerial haze that helps make the set seem bigger."

**"I loved the scanning room we used on the pilot, which was one thing we didn't use as much during the season,"** DP Michael Bonvillain says. **"I was kind of hoping we'd use it more. It reminded me of a visual and psychological reference from the shows I saw as a kid, like the tape recorder that self-destructed on *Mission: Impossible*. The scanning room seemed like it'd be such a cool signature for *Alias*, something kids watching today would remember twenty years from now."**

Sydney, Dixon, and Sloane convene in the SD-6 conference room. According to Michael Bonvillain, the color palette, achieved through lights, stage smoke, camera filters, and other tricks, helped distinguish the show's various environments. "SD-6 has the cutting-edge technology," Bonvillain explains. "We wanted that place to look slicker in contrast with the CIA, which is more drab, with older, uglier computers."

The insidious world of SD-6, that subterranean realm below the Credit Dauphine bank building, was also designed to sharply contrast with the CIA's Los Angeles–based bureau. "While SD-6 would be super sleek with very advanced technology, we wanted to create a CIA environment that reinforced the idea of governmental bureaucracy," explained production designer Scott Chambliss, another member of the *Alias* creative team from the pilot. "Our CIA was definitely not going to be a hip place, but we didn't do a *Doctor Strangelove* on them. The CIA today is very '80s industrial park and utterly bland, but we gave it the retro personality of the CIA from the 1950s and '60s."

Chambliss's department was a large one, including an art director, set designer, research assistant, a graphics assistant, and more employees for set decoration, prop making, construction and paint, and on-set work. The department's ambitious agenda was to design and build the permanent and changing (or "swing") sets and even transform off-the-lot locations into any scripted environment.

## BUILDING THE WORLD

"Even though we implied a world in the pilot, we didn't build the whole world," Chambliss explained, "but we built it for the series. For example, for the SD-6 set I had to design and create a ground plan and a flow and places that could play as different types of spaces depending on what the story needed, creating the impression that this place went on and on. The concept of SD-6 remained constant from the pilot, the idea of this safe and solid place deep underground furnished with all this cold, advanced technological equipment. Visually, this is what worked best for me on the show."

Jack Bristow takes a meeting in the SD-6 conference room. "I've done so many scenes in the SD-6 office and conference room set that it's a comfort zone for me," says Victor Garber. "It's a really good set and such a great crew that when you're filming there it feels very complete and real. It's not hard to put yourself in that situation [of actually being in SD-6]."

A disappointment for Chambliss, and part of the reality of having to create a world on a budget for a first-season show still having to prove itself, was the cost-saving consolidation of the CIA and newspaper offices into one interchangeable set. Another idea lost in the transition from concept to construction blueprints was "this really groovy bar-restaurant-hangout thing," as Chambliss called it, for

Marshall unveils yet another of his marvelous gadgets—no SD-6 mission is complete without one. "I think SD-6 puts up with Marshall's bumbling nature because he comes up with kick-ass stuff, can crack encryption codes, knows computers—he's a genius," says Kevin Weisman. "So they allow for his tangents, although sometimes Sloane will snap at me, 'Marshall, get back to the point.'"

**"The writers will have a rough idea of a Marshall gadget and I'll figure out what it can be and how it can work," explains technical consultant Rick Orci. "It's all theoretical, but we try to base the gadgets on reality."**

Sydney and her friends. The hangout was designed but scrapped when "story needs changed," Chambliss explained. "At the beginning, it looked like our show was going to have a lot more of the qualities of *Felicity*."

Although the spy intrigues drove most of the plot in each episode, the personal side of Sydney's life remained a key aspect of the series. In the first season, the main environment for that domestic side was Sydney's house, which she'd share with Francie after her break-up with Charlie.

"Working in television is a double-edged sword—the thing I like about it is also

Sloane confers with his British counterpart, SD-9 head Edward Poole, who later betrays the SD-6 leader. DP Bonvillain reveals he loves lighting Ron Rifkin, particularly the actor's eyes, to reflect Sloane's sinister aspect.

"Michael is obsessed with lighting me and I don't know why," Rifkin chuckles. "I've never felt so protected and taken care of."

what I dislike," Chambliss concluded. "I love how, especially on this show, you have to create vivid environments in shorthand. But what I'm not thrilled about is that the TV screen is so small you don't see the level of detail you'd have on feature films—even the permanent sets aren't at the level of what they'd be on my movie work. But what's also good about this show is we're going for maximum vividness."

## COSTUME DESIGN

Laura Goldsmith, a costume designer who'd worked in features (including *Leaving Las Vegas*), missed the pilot but was aboard for the rest of the season. Goldsmith echoed some of Chambliss's first-season blues, explaining that big costume departments and full-time seamstresses were blessings "that come with time and success and longevity. When you go into a season you don't really know what it's going to bring; you can only base it on the pilot."

Unlike designing costumes for film, working at the hectic pace of episodic television didn't allow for concept sketches and paintings. "I didn't do one drawing on this show. There wasn't enough time. A lot of times I pulled tear sheets from magazines, got a fabric sample or color and texture ideas, combining things to get what I wanted."

As with the design of environments, there was a master plan for the clothes worn by the characters. The wardrobe at SD-6 was heavy on black and white and grays to match the cold, steely surroundings—past the scanning room below Credit Dauphine, there are no warm colors, like brown or beige. In contrast was the warmer color palette and conservative dress of the CIA office. The newspaper office also drew from the warmer side of the spectrum while emphasizing casual dress: jeans and slacks, corduroys and blazers.

As the first season wrapped, Laura Goldsmith had artist Felipe Sanchez render artwork of some of her distinctive designs for Sydney's aliases. (Note: The production numbering system, as marked on the artwork, began at #631 for the season's second episode. The third episode, "Parity," was numbered 632, and so on.)

EPISODE
631

*Alias*
Sydney

Costumes By:*
Laura Goldsmith

Felipe Sanchez 5.7.2002

The blue party dress from "So It Begins."

Costumes By:
Laura Goldsmith

Alias
Sydney

*AdrioSanchez 5.1.2002*

A design for Sydney as she elegantly swings into action in the "Parity" episode.

EPISODE
635

Alias
Sydney

Costumes By:
Laura Goldsmith

Aslyee Sanchez 5·1·2002

In "Reckoning," Agent Dixon posed as a wealthy art buyer while Sydney, as his girl-friend, wore this sexy green number.

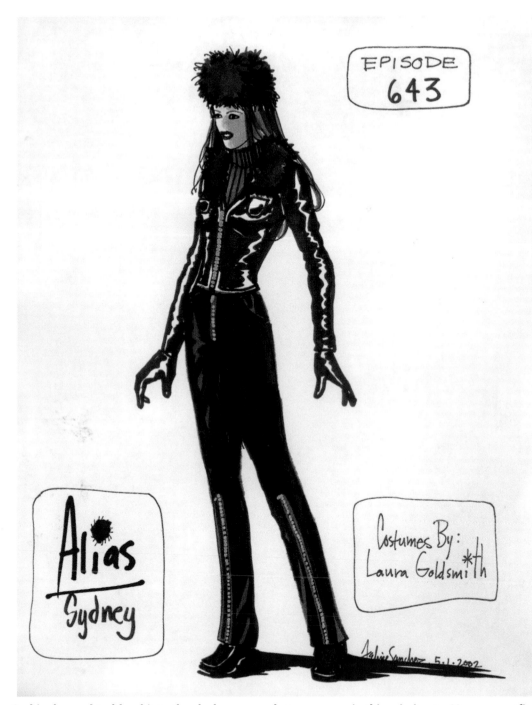

Alias
Sydney

Costumes By:
Laura Goldsmith

Jackie Sanchez 5.1.2002

Syd is dressed to blend into the darkness—and stay warm—in this mission-to-Moscow outfit for "The Coup."

EPISODE
650

Alias
Sydney

TAILORED
TUXEDO

Costumes by:
Laura Goldsmith *4/

FelipeSanchez 5-1-2002

**This stylish, form-fitting Paris-cabaret ensemble for "Rendezvous" allowed Syd to kick butt and save Will—and look good doing it.**

EPISODE
651

ALÍAS

SYD

Costumes:
Laura Goldsmith

Trashy but classy. Sydney's outfit for a Taipai "fetish club" in "Almost 30 Years," the first season's final episode.

**Dixon poses as a wealthy art lover and Sydney his indulged girlfriend, in another of their SD-6 aliases.**

Ever resourceful, Goldsmith tapped into a network of major clothing stores, small designers, and dress shops, ranging from chain stores to L.A.'s own Trashy Lingerie. She got many of reporter Will's classic "old school jackets" at Banana Republic, which allowed her to purchase the multiples that might be needed.

Sydney Bristow's fashions, of course, were an integral part of the show's style and sense of fun. "We figured that since Sydney's missions and her aliases were so theatrical and accessorized, it'd be best to uncomplicate her SD-6 and student life and make that clean and simple," Goldsmith explained. "Like everyone at SD-6, her clothes are classic, but when she's at home, it's denim shorts or a Calvin Klein tank top. I avoided anything that was a fad and might look dated. I try to keep it timeless with her.

"The costumes for her aliases were all challenging. There are two kinds of missions she goes on: Some are glamorous and seductive, where she kicks butt, and there are tactical missions, where she might be climbing up a building while wearing gear. If she's going to a different terrain I try to factor that into the locale or be cinematic—a khaki palette if she's going to Australia, or maybe a black leather Berlin look for a mission in Germany."

But no matter the costume, from French maid outfits to elegant gowns and one notably skintight blue dress, Garner remained sexy but elegant—an Audrey Hepburn with a smashing roundhouse kick. "Jennifer has this incredible allure, the ability to not look trashy even when wearing trashy things." Goldsmith smiled. "That quality comes from her. She makes it happen."

# THE CAST ASSEMBLES

In TV land "pilot season" is a hopeful time for a prospective series and begins with scripts and character breakdowns sent to agents on behalf of their actor clients. For the actors it's a shoe-leather process of going to casting calls, meeting producers and directors, auditioning, and hopefully reaching the Promised Land of the coveted part.

A major villain of the pilot, who would return in the season's final episode, was the Taiwanese torturer known in the script only as Suit and Glasses. The role went to Ric Young, an actor who had played everything from a Red Guard interrogator in *The Last Emperor* to Chairman Mao in *Nixon*. "When I read the script I thought, Wow, what a script!" Young grinned. "You get television scripts that have a certain formula, but this one had twists and turns, it had me riveted. And my character was not so much about dialogue but the journey this man is going through. I was determined to get the part and lucky enough that J.J. cast me and gave me so many wonderful moments. He allowed me to really live in my head and let the camera be there."

For the key role of Jack Bristow, Sydney's father, an early rumor was that the production was interested in Donald Sutherland. Ultimately, Ron Rifkin and Victor Garber, two stage and screen stars, read for the parts of both Jack and SD-6 leader Arvin Sloane. "I was so intrigued by the writing and the characters that I felt if I was going to get involved in a television series, then this would be the one," Garber recalled. "But the role of Jack interested me the most, because of the father and daughter relationship, so that was the one I auditioned for.

"The character of Jack is so multi-dimensional and well written that he's fun to do. Working in television or film is obviously different from the stage, but no matter the medium, I approach every role I do in the same way—what is the truth for me in this situation? Then you go from there. A nice thing about *Alias* is each episode takes you in different directions, as opposed to a play, which is the same every night. That's the fun, that the story expands and evolves each week."

Although Ron Rifkin read for the Jack Bristow part, J. J. Abrams insisted he play Sloane. Rifkin got into the character by molding the look of the SD-6 leader. "I'd worn a beard in a play I did called *The Substance of Fire* [which won Rifkin an Obie and other stage awards] and also in the movie adaptation, and I sort of liked the idea of a beard for Sloane. When we were doing the

Sydney, in that famous red wig from the pilot episode, enters the Los Angeles CIA bureau. This lobby scene was staged at the Los Angeles Center Studios, a production facility. When the show won a series run, the production could build its own permanent sets.

Sydney and her CIA handler, Vaughn, take a meeting posing as joggers taking a breather. Their attraction for each other is tempered by protocol forbidding romance between agent and handler. "Michael is so intense, very focused and contained," Garner says of Vartan. "He can do these quiet, longing looks like no one else on the planet."

pilot I said to J.J. that I really wanted to go against the grain; you think of FBI or CIA people as being clean shaven and I'd like to have a bit of a beard. And he said, 'Go for it!' It was the right choice for me. I also have a lot of input in terms of the way I dress on the show. All my clothes are by this one guy in New York, John Varvatos, and it's very specific: Sloane's jacket is never open, his ties are always just so, the collars are very neat. Then, when we see Sloane at home, I decided to wear glasses. In the office I wear contacts, but it's only in my home that I relax a bit."

Kevin Weisman recalled that when he received the character breakdown for Marshall, the SD-6 gadget wizard was described as an ex-hippie computer programmer/hacker in his late forties. "I'm none of those things," Weisman laughed. The actor, who had a recurring role on Abrams's *Felicity*, huddled with Abrams and came up with a character that would be just as unlike him as that hippie hacker: a certifiable high-tech genius noticeably lacking in social skills, whose overheated mind was prone to tangents.

Merrin Dungey had a similar opportunity to work with Abrams on the character of Francie, Sydney Bristow's best friend. "It was pilot season

Will Tippin, aka Bradley Cooper, at his desk at the newspaper office (which also doubled as the CIA office the first season). When Abrams couldn't get permission to present Tippin's newspaper as the *Los Angeles Times*, he decided not to name the paper, rather than creating a fake one.

The illusion of a world outside the windows of this and other soundstage sets was created with city skyline photos blown up as 30 x 40-foot translights, or tracing paper covering the windows and backlit for an overexposed, sunlit effect.

and *Alias* was one of the best scripts I'd read," recalled Dungey. "I had an initial meeting with J.J. and we hit it off, it was really clicking, which doesn't always happen. We were trying to figure out how Francie was supposed to feel about Sydney's engagement with respect to her own boyfriend and how to play that."

Dungey noted that the show's balancing act between Sydney's secret-agent activities and her private life actually gave credibility to the show's sometimes fantastical situations. "Isn't that the point, that CIA agents and people who really are sent out on missions have private lives, take their families to Disneyland? It puts a face on the agents that are out there serving our country. The James Bond films were always exciting, but you'd care a bit more if you felt that was a real human being. But instead of suspending your disbelief on this show, you care so much more about Sydney because you see her personal life. So you're worried when she's rappelling down a building or being shot at. She's not genetically engineered, she's not some superhero who's always going to win."

"Dixon is a man of the world and seemed to have all sorts of possibilities," Carl Lumbly recalled of the role of Sydney's SD-6 partner. "I also found it intriguing to play a patriot. I am of a generation that came out of protest, the civil rights and anti–Vietnam War movements. In Dixon's case, he came out of that experience with a love for the possibilities of the country and the desire to defend it with everything, including his life. I thought it'd be fun to play someone who knows they're right and feels so single-minded about it."

To get into Agent Dixon's head, Lumbly followed his normal process of creating a back story for his character. "Creating a show is such a massive piece of machinery, and I believe in playing the page [of the script], so I generally keep this back story to myself," Lumbly explained. "I feel that's how we all carry our history, anyway—you have all these facts about who you are, but you don't lay that out to someone unless you're comfortable or feel the need."

Although the production had permanent and "swing" sets, it regularly went on location in the greater Los Angeles area. The home of Arvin and Emily Sloane, where this dinner party scene is set, was actually the historic Dorothy Chandler house.

Lumbly envisioned Dixon as coming out of the black middle class, with a father in the military and a mother who was an educator. His parents wanted him to become an attorney, but after losing his student deferment Dixon was profoundly affected by being drafted and serving in Vietnam. "In my back story, Dixon has this hyperactive nature of going mountain biking and playing rac-

**At the dinner party, Sloane shows Sydney his copy of the Rambaldi manuscript, one of the artifacts of the Renaissance scientist and seer coveted by rival spy agencies.**

quetball. After leaving SD-6 at the end of his work day, Dixon has to go and release. As an agent he can't have a regular therapist and he certainly wants to have as little to do with McCullough [feared SD-6 interrogator, played by Angus Scrimm] as possible, so he has his own meditational process. I think there's a spiritual side to Dixon that he's very, very quiet about. All of that, I feel, feeds his seemingly calm demeanor."

When casting for CIA agent Vaughn, Abrams thought of Michael Vartan, an actor who'd been in his film *The Pallbearer*. Despite his successes, Vartan has a self-deprecating take on his profession: "I have no idea what acting is and I didn't get into this because I love acting. It was just that I was broke and said to myself, 'Okay, I'll try acting.' Honestly, I don't know what I did for *Alias* that I didn't do in other auditions. Don't get me wrong, I love my job. But it's all a whim and if the stars align it's 'Hallelujah,' and if they don't, you move on."

Vartan had to persevere through, as he described, years of three or four rejections a week and starving-artist jobs ranging from running errands for a record company to working a deli counter. When Vartan first moved to Los Angeles, he also haunted the area's pool halls and parlors. He'd enjoyed playing pool as a kid and realized he had a knack for playing for money, and he came to know the thrill of having thousands of dollars riding on a shot.

"You just show up at a pool hall and within ten minutes you get a couple sharks circling your table," he said with a smile, adding that he probably broke even during his playing days. "If you're good you can make a penny and if you suck, then you shouldn't be playing for money. People think it's just a game, but it's intense. It doesn't work like they've shown it in movies like *The Color of Money*, the romance of it—there are guys who end up in trash cans outside pool halls, stabbed to death.

"But you definitely meet some interesting characters. One of my mentors was a guy they called The Drummer. He happened to be one of Frank Sinatra's first studio musicians way before Frank got famous. He played drums in this early studio session. That's how he got his name, The Drummer. He's an eighty-year-old guy who chain smokes, has every cancer known to man, shakes like a leaf—but, boy, can he play. The Drummer taught me that if you're mentally sharp you can beat someone more talented. But I haven't played in about five years. It became like a drug to me, so I had to step away from the pool halls."

When Bradley Cooper came on as Will he related to the character's reportorial career—as a teenager he'd dreamed of becoming a journalist. Bradley also got into the mindset of Will's look, which evoked the Watergate era of *All the President's Men*. "I saw Will as sort of a throwback to the seventies," Cooper observed. "It's such a high-tech show with all the cutting-edge gadgetry, and Will is this guy dressed in corduroy and glasses who has the pen and notepad, the pocket protector kind of thing."

When Cooper came out to Los Angeles to shoot the series pilot, he dived into the reporter's world by shadowing a *Los Angeles Times* reporter during a heady, pressure-filled L.A. mayoral campaign. Cooper noticed that the reporter he was following had a desk that was "this centrifuge of food coming in and out. You have no time to eat but you're constantly under stress and running around, so food is a necessity, of course. It was amazing to watch this reporter constantly eating bagels, leaving around half-empty cups of coffee, half-eaten

The show's key hairstylist, Michael Reitz, designed and styled the wigs supplied by Hollywood veteran Renate Leuschner. "Michael is a key element. Wigs are a big part of a look—the most important item, I think," says costumer Laura Goldsmith. "You can have gorgeous young actors, but if you screw up the hair it ruins everything, it ruins the outfit."

sandwiches like carcasses on his desk amidst all this paperwork. So that insight was a wonderful thing I integrated that informs the psychology of my character."

For Jennifer Garner, her success as series lead was a case of the overnight sensation that was years in the making. "I've been the lead in Hallmark movies and a million different stage productions," she noted. "It's never bothered me to have a smaller or bigger role. It didn't in college (Denison University in Ohio), where I'd sometimes audition for smaller roles because they can be more fun. When I studied acting in college I wasn't the most talented person there—but I was the hungriest. It's about working and continuing to work. I can put myself in the structure of something, and if I have more responsibility in a show that's great, if it's a smaller role then fine, that's what I'm going to do, it doesn't matter to me. I think what prepared me for this role was that I've been around for years and done different kinds of work. Plus, life itself prepares you."

What intrigued Garner about Sydney Bristow was the character's complexity. "Sydney had a loneliness and desperation about her, and this desire to be normal. I'm not lonely and I am normal, but you connect with some roles more than others, and this one clicked the moment I got [the pilot script]. As crazy as some of the things that happen to Sydney are, J.J. makes them believable to me. I think it's so in the script. If what's been written is believable, then it's not hard to play. The pilot was so beautifully written, and everything she said sounded like something that I could say, and that's just a gift that J.J. has, whether he's writing for the action world of *Armageddon* or the relationship world of *Felicity*. He can look at everything as a whole and see how changing some detail would alter things fourteen episodes later."

Garner also brought an athleticism to go with her acting skills. To keep in shape over the season's marathon run, she adhered to a demanding regimen designed by her trainer, which ranged from early-morning runs for cardiovascular strength to scheduled workouts with weights and abdominal and leg exercises. "People always say to me, 'Your character is so great because it keeps you in shape.' Actually, it's the opposite of that—I have to stay in shape to be this character. I might be in an action sequence where I have to hang and hold my own weight and pull myself up and down. Doing that once is no big deal, but in the course of shooting an action sequence you might have to do that twenty times. So I have to have the strength to sustain that. It's so important to me to do my own [stunts] and that I have fun doing it."

As the series star, Garner earned raves from the rest of the cast for her unselfish acceptance of the burdens of being the lead, for a superb work ethic, and for a natural leadership quality that acknowledged without words that she was, in the final analysis, part of a whole. "We shoot faster than you can imagine, so I show up and do what the director tells me." Garner grinned. "I'm inspired by everything around me, what the set creators and my hair and makeup people come up with—they all create a world I get to step into.

"The best part is everything that exists in this world, that one thing isn't better than the other. If I'm tired of doing action sequences, I can have a beautiful dramatic scene with Victor, or if I'm exhausted after too many emotional scenes, there'll be a fun scene with Merrin and Bradley. I feel like an apprentice to all these actors that I look up to and believe in and want to be like. Because I work with Carl I listen better in a scene than I used to, with Victor I'm more still, with Ron I'm more easy with my body movements. That's the gift the show has given me."

The world of *Alias* is a haunting one, Garner concluded. "You don't play a spy without suddenly looking at the world differently, wondering if someone is really who they say they are, or if a certain situation is as easy as it looks. Are there safe houses everywhere? I'd never thought about those things before. We all kind of accept what we're exposed to. I don't have a dark view, but it's just knowing that there's more out there than meets the eye—and what is it?"

# PROP AND DRAPE

Writer's assistant Sean Gerace, on another leg of the *Alias* world tour, noted that in addition to the soundstage sets, a remarkable number of locations never left the grounds of the Disney/ABC lot. For example, in the basement of Disney's Property and Drapery Building is the secret meeting place most often used when Sydney received her CIA counter-missions from Agent Vaughn. Identified in scripts as the "mikro storage" area, this rendezvous is at the far end of a labyrinthine underground area of long aisles and storage cages stocked with furniture and heavy items.

Back upstairs in Prop and Drape, it's the ultimate attic, a cavernous space where all the fun stuff used on Disney TV and features is stored and rented out to other productions: the spotted couch from the live-action *101 Dalmatians* and other iconic and recognizable props, rows of coffins and Egyptian sarcophaguses, hanging skeletons and mannequins, weird tribal masks and antique clocks and period pieces. "A couple years ago they'd unloaded all the property from *The 13th Warrior*, an Antonio Banderas movie, and when I came in, I was horrified." Gerace shuddered. "They had all these dismembered corpses hanging from the ceiling. They were fakes, of course, but it still felt like I'd walked into a charnel house."

Around the corner from Prop and Drape was the storage shed where the props created during the show's twenty-two-episode season were stored. At season's end, they'd wind up in the vast rooms and storage cages of Prop and Drape, but for now, in the middle of the first season, the artifacts were collected in the shelves and boxes of this roughly twenty-by-forty-foot storage space. "If Marshall had a back room, this would be it," says Christopher Call, the *Alias* property master brought on by Scott

Bitter ex-SD-6 agent McKenas Cole taunts a captured Arvin Sloane with the container holding the exotic "needles of fire," a memorable item produced by property master Christopher Call.

Chambliss. "Basically, a prop is anything the actor picks up, carries, touches, or moves around, and even set pieces scripted for action. The ongoing joke from the writers is 'small black device,' meaning some Marshall gadget for opening a safe or breaking into a room."

The mystical page 47 of the Rambaldi manuscript, with its likeness of Sydney Bristow, made the double agent an early suspect as the bringer of the dread Prophecy. This and all Rambaldi art were actually the work of artist Andrea Dietrich, who was brought onto the production by Sarah Caplan.

# "NEEDLES OF FIRE"
## AND OTHER ARTIFACTS

Call's responsibilities were twofold: After designing the props (usually with the help of Abrams, the writers, and sometimes the production designer and the current episode's director), he had to produce them—usually three to seven individual items per episode. Some were found objects picked up at favorite haunts, from flea markets to quick trips to Prop and Drape. But most *Alias* props were manufactured by outside vendors.

"I've been doing prop work in Los Angeles for about seven years, and when you find guys who are truly obsessed by what they're doing, you hold on to them," Call said. "There's Tony Swatton at Sword and the Stone here in Burbank. I don't know when he ever sleeps. Everybody goes to him because he's so good; his face is always blackened from being in the back of his shop hammering out steel. The same thing with the guys at Neotek, a nearby manufacturer I use a lot—I couldn't do the show without them. I could call Neotek at six-thirty in the morning or six-thirty in the evening and there'd be somebody there working. I might say, 'Guys, we need this and it plays in two days.' I'll explain it or give them a drawing, walk away, and when it's needed—there it is.

"For one episode [18, "Masquerade"] I needed to build a robotic arm, which can cost thirty thousand dollars, but I found Mark Pollock, this colorful guy in the Valley from Flix FX, Inc., who actually had a robotic arm up in the rafters of his place! It was in disrepair, but he threw it down, dusted it off, and said, 'I can make it work again!' And he did; it came off looking great."

On every shelf and corner of the storage shed was an item—and a story. There was a photo of Jennifer Garner's character sitting in front of a "Happy Birthday, Sydney" banner, the image that jogged the repressed memory of Martin Shepard, Danny's programmed assassin in "Color-Blind." There was one of those "small black devices," a circular object, complete with flashing light display and magnetic backing, which Jack Bristow once used to tap into SD-6 computers. Here was the baseball-sized sphere that served as the nuclear core Sydney stole from arms dealer Ineni Hassan. There was a syringe Neotek outfitted with a fake internal chamber and a retractable needle, which was almost used on Sydney during an SD-6 interrogation.

On a shelf was the seat-belt-buckle-shaped USB computer port housing that Neotek modified with an electronic display "progress bar" for the safecracking device used in "The Box." There was also Sloane's severed finger. In the storyline Sloane, bound and tied, orders Jack Bristow to cut off his finger and use the fingerprint to deactivate an SD-6 fail-safe device. Sloane's finger was subsequently reattached, leaving this foam finger as a grisly souvenir of the episode.

Inside a metallic suitcase that looked like something Sydney might grab were other *Alias* artifacts, notably the container for the deadly "needles of fire" that Quentin Tarantino's McKenas Cole used to torture a captured Sloane. "I had fun making this," Call related, "because it seemed old and scary to me. This was a rare find. I got this out of the Disney prop house."

Call had known at the outset that the box holding the "needles of fire" needed a nineteenth-century look, and he knew Prop and Drape had an eclectic selection of boxes of all makes, sizes, and shapes. "I don't know what it was originally used for," he said, picking up the small, exotic-looking container. "I believe it was designed to hold mechanical pencils and drafting tools. But when I found it, I was elated. It seemed the perfect thing for an episode titled 'The Box.'"

The oblong container had two carrying straps, which, Call demonstrated, were wrapped around each end to make it seem even more threatening—*There's something inside we can't let out.* He opened it and inside was a rolled-up cloth. "I bought a piece of fabric that was the size of a tablecloth, just to cut off and fray the edges for this eighteen-by-eight-inch piece. The needles were originally supposed to be loose in the box, but I came up with the idea of this cloth. Quentin really got to play with that, teasing Sloane by opening the box, then pulling out this rolled-up cloth—yet another layer of suspense to unravel."

Sewn in the center of the cloth was a patch of leather with ten needles affixed, one of them retractable for the moment when a needle is inserted into Sloane's hand. "Each needle is supposed to be more intense than the last one," Call said. "Which side is the most intense? It never got that far. Only Quentin Tarantino knows for sure, and he's not talking."

Call carefully rolled up the needles, closed the box, and stored it away. He walked to the back of the storage room. Stacked on a shelf were the breakaway balsa-wood hymnal posts used in a fight scene in a Catholic church between Sydney and Anna Espinosa, her rival from K-Directorate, one of the mysterious spy agencies competing for Rambaldi artifacts with the CIA, SD-6, and other clandestine organiztions. On the adjacent shelf was the object for which they were fighting—the sun-colored oval from the church's stained-glass window. It wasn't revealed at that time, but this was the missing piece for an old clock made to the specifications of Renaissance scientist and seer Milo Rambaldi.

A major plotline was the race between rival spy agencies for Rambaldi artifacts, scattered puzzle pieces of a bigger picture—perhaps a technology or a hidden truth—that would rock the modern world. They could have saved themselves the globe-trotting trouble—Rambaldi's artifacts were here, scattered about this room all the time.

# THE RAMBALDI ARTIFACTS

On a shelf by the back wall was the Rambaldi clock, complete with heavy brass base and a delicate meshing of gears, an intricate prop Neotek created in ten days. "It's a work of art. They outdid themselves on this one," Call said as he lifted it from the shelf. He pointed out the mystical Rambaldi symbol <0> etched into the works and indicated where the stained-glass piece was inserted, noting how the clock was powered by hidden D-cell batteries. "To make it look aged we had it oxidized, a patina process. It's like a green paint that when applied to brass gives it an aged look."

Near the entrance was the Rambaldi painting of Pope Alexander VI that Sydney and Vaughn located in the Vatican vaults. The painting pictured the Pope gesturing toward a stream of script along the borders—Rambaldi code opening another door into the mystery known as the Prophecy. The painting, Call explained, was the work of freelance artist Andrea Dietrich. "For all intents and purposes, she is Rambaldi. She does all the Rambaldi artwork."

Call pulled out a leather-bound manuscript—the coveted fifteenth-century Rambaldi manuscript. The pages lay inside a handmade leather case etched with the <0> symbol for the Magnific Order of Rambaldi. The book was scripted to be thrown by Sydney during a struggle with the irrepressible Anna, so Call suggested securing the manuscript in a leather case so pages

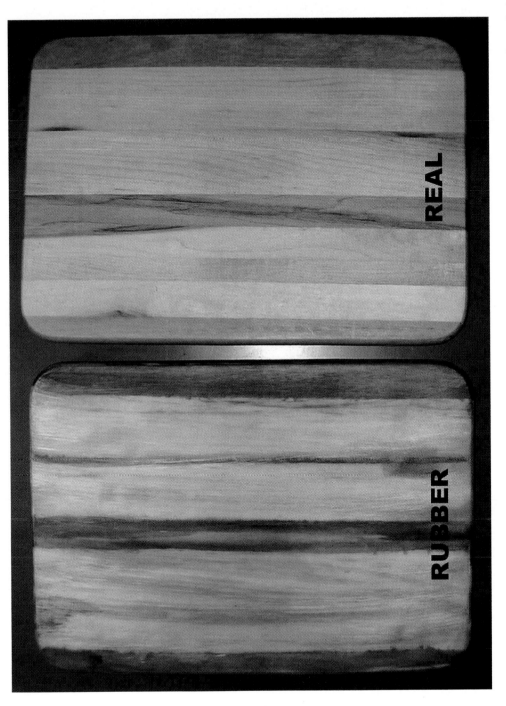

REAL

RUBBER

"Here's a cutting board Jennifer used in the kitchen fight for episode nineteen ["Snowman"]," Call says. "Neotek made it out of rubber, and when they were filming, one of the stunt guys goes, 'Oh, this is great! I can take this in the face!'—Spoken like a true stunt guy."

wouldn't fly apart. Abrams liked the idea, and Tony at Sword and the Stone fashioned it.

Call opened the case to reveal the manuscript pages: There was the drawing of the Rambaldi clock on one page, the design for a globe-shaped device on another. The top sheet was the mystical page forty-seven, complete with the portrait of a woman revealed by the wash from the SD-6 vault, obtained by the CIA when they captured McKenas Cole. It's the haunting face of the apocalyptic Prophecy described in the mystic Rambaldi codes.

"This is all Andrea's work," Call said, lifting pages designed to look like the manuscripts of Leonardo da Vinci. "The pages are parchment she treated and aged."

As the leather case closed on the Rambaldi manuscript, Sloane's words seemed to echo in the room: "Men would die for this book. Men have died."

DOUBLE LIFE

It's the classic opener for a TV adventure series: An intrepid squad of heroes receives that week's dangerous assignment, which, of course, will be successfully completed before the final commercial. In *Alias*, that convention gets turned on its head—SD-6 agents and their missions are in opposition to America. "It does make the audience stop: 'Oh, this SD-6 mission is not what we want, they have to be defeated,' " Abrams reflected. "So each SD-6 mission needs a [CIA] countermission. The story is not just about Sydney Bristow, girl spy, but about her being a double agent—and the possibilities of that increase exponentially."

As a university grad student she dreams of becoming a teacher like her dear, departed mom (that is, before learning that her KGB-agent mother's whole family life was an alias).

The show's other compelling (or vexing) aspect is that the storytelling terrain is not brightly lit and easily followed—*Alias* is a shadow land of secrets, even to crew and cast members, who often don't know the upcoming twists and turns until they read the script. "Part of the fun of the series is everything isn't spelled out, and even when we answer some questions we're raising new ones," Abrams observed. "But I respect the audience and believe they'll understand our stories without having all the answers.

"You can simply go for the eye candy and obvious intrigue of this girl who goes on spy missions. But if you watch the show, you can quickly understand and relate to

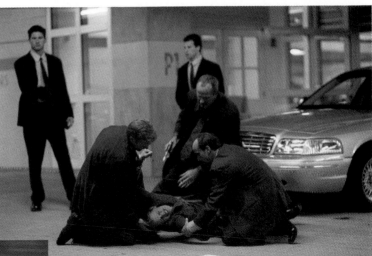

As a double agent, Sydney skates a thin line at all times. Suspected of being a traitorous mole inside SD-6, she's captured and endures the hot seat.

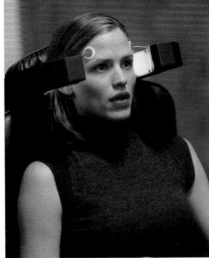

Sydney's emotional state. There's questions about Sydney's mother and father, this forbidden relationship with Agent Vaughn, questions about what Sloane knows about her and why he cares for her. Those questions are a layer deeper than that first level of the beautiful girl going on missions and leading a double life. The third layer is anticipating things and asking questions, getting to understand the different players in this world. It's sort of like quicksand—if you get into it, you'll sink into the depths of it."

## PRIVATE STORIES

As a Los Angeles grad student with an intimate circle of friends, Sydney has all the trappings of a normal life. On most TV shows, that would be a cardboard world, quickly discarded to get to Sydney's secret action-hero persona and those kick-ass spy missions. But *Alias* in its first season let viewers into Sydney's domestic circle with scenes of friends at home playing board games or drinking wine and shooting the breeze, enjoying a Halloween costume party or celebrating Thanksgiving dinner. "I love those moments that aren't plot driven, that we don't always have her pulled away from dinner with her friends to a mission," said writer Roberto Orci. "We want her to interact with her friends and not just the spy world, to make those moments believable."

But the undeniable tension of Sydney's dual lives had to be accounted for, with the writers scripting dawning suspicions among Sydney's friends about her obsession with that all-consuming job at the bank. "There's the episode after I'd broken up with my boyfriend that I turn on Sydney, letting her know that her not always being there for me has not gone unnoticed," Merrin Dungey said of Francie. "I'm not just some weak character."

It was Dungey who talked out with J. J. Abrams the problems inherent in Francie's romance with Charlie, heading off one of the major plotlines— at one point the season-ending episode was going to include the wedding of Francie and Charlie, Dungey explained. "Francie needed something else to happen in her story line because if she married Charlie, what would happen with her relationship with Sydney? If I'm married and having kids while she's off on missions, it'd splinter our friendship, it'd be a constant reflection of the things Sydney doesn't have. Now, I think my character will get stronger and be more a part of Sydney's world."

Will Tippin, one of the pivotal figures in Sydney's private life, provided an underlying and ongoing tension as his investigation of Danny's death unwittingly drew him closer to Sydney's secret. A potential end for the character was established in the form of David McNeil (played by executive producer and regular episode director Ken Olin), a man in prison whose wife was killed because he'd gotten too close to SD-6.

An early red flag to a truth-seeking journalist like Will was his discovery in episode 2, "So It Begins," that Danny had been booked on a flight to Singapore the night of his murder (Jack Bristow's last-ditch attempt to save his daughter's

"I don't think having all the answers is necessarily a good thing," says creator J. J. Abrams. "I don't think this story would work as well if we were too literal. For me, the scariest monster is the one that you don't see, or only see bits of."

future husband). That scene, episode director Ken Olin noted, was "a breakthrough" for both Jennifer Garner and him, coming as it did so early in the season, at a time when Sydney (and all the characters) was still being fleshed out and coming to life. "Jennifer didn't know how her character should be emotional even though it was important to convince Will to back off the story," Olin said of the scene. "Jennifer is part of a generation of actors who place a high value on emotional truth—but Sydney doesn't have to be one hundred percent emotionally honest. [As a spy] she has to do crazy things. We came to the point where it was okay that Sydney lies. She sometimes puts on an act, which is difficult for her emotionally. That insight was so liberating for Jennifer."

"She makes Will feel bad about telling her about the ticket [to Singapore], but at the same time the viewer knows she's hiding who she really is,"

Cooper added. "When Will turned around, the camera stayed on Sydney and you saw that double-agent look. That light-switch change, emotionally, is how the character navigated the rest of the season of having to constantly be different things for different people.

The seminal pilot scene of Sydney Bristow, determined to bring down SD-6, writing down a statement detailing everything she knows for CIA agents Vaughn and Weiss (Greg Grunberg). Abrams, who wrote the pilot, realized while scripting this scene that there was the possibility for an ongoing romantic tension between Bristow and Vaughn.

"Being in that scene with such a talented actress, for me, was a lesson in where I really need to be as an actor. Jennifer didn't play that scene in one note, she was able to color it in three different stages. The first is her compassion for Will, the next is she's taking in information, trying to figure out what else Will knows—Sydney didn't know about that flight to Singapore—and then she fakes it, saying she knew Danny was booked on that flight but couldn't go with him. Playing all those different things at the same time is very hard to do."

"The amazing thing was we had to learn how to make Sydney manipulative," Garner concluded. "It's hard to play Sydney faking emotions, but you simply play that as honestly as you can. I'm into what's best for the scene. I can do one hundred percent emotion and I'll go there. But there was a scene in the pilot where I was supposed to have a completely straight face, with tears rolling down my face, and we used a blower in my eyes, rather than doing it the way I'd cry in real life, with me squinching my face. That taught me a lot. It's not always about reaching into your gut and twisting it up."

The recurring poignant character of cancer-stricken Emily Sloane (Amy Irving) shows us a new side of Arvin Sloane. Her husband's love and compassion for her make Sloane more than a cardboard bad guy.

That Will would, by season's end, become drawn into the shadowy world of espionage was an effort to make him a major player in Sydney's double life and even more of a romantic possibility than the early "best friends" scenario. "Since many of the viewers were finding Will annoying and not this great guy, we decided to clue him in on her secret in time for the next season," Alexander explained. "The other interesting part of that was to make Will a realistic rival [of Vaughn] for Sydney's affections. Vaughn is looking out for Sydney, but as her handler at the CIA he's involved in all the protocol and responsibilities of that world. But Will only cares about Sydney."

John Eisendrath noted that during those sessions in the writers' room to break each episode, the first item on the agenda was always Sydney's personal stories, one of the most important of which was the relationship with her father. "The relationship between Sydney and Jack was clearly integral to the pilot," Eisendrath explained, "and so much the fulcrum of the show the first year. It was a great tether to reality and to where we'd go into this fantastical spy world."

Jack Bristow's burdens are heavy ones—betrayed by a wife who was a KGB agent, he lives the life of a double agent while worrying about the safety of his own double-agent daughter. But over the journey of the season, father and daughter would become closer. "Overall, there's been an interesting arc for my character," Garber observed. "When I first started, people watching the show would stop me and ask why I was being so mean to Sydney. 'Why are you such a bad father?' I said, 'Don't worry, it'll change.'"

Of course, while father and daughter became more united in their shared purpose to bring down SD-6, they were still working under the omnipresent shadow of Sloane. Sloane is a complex figure who, like Sydney, has a private life, notably a beautiful wife (played by Amy Irving) facing a battle with cancer. "Sloane is not just a cardboard villain," Abrams added. "He can have someone killed and yet, when his wife's new medication is giving her pain, he can kiss her on the forehead and be there for her. Although he's a villain, you can sympathize with him. He can even be manipulated."

At home, best friends Sydney and Francie prepare for a party. "In the beginning I was like, 'Francie will turn a gun on Sydney and become a crazy spy!'" laughs Merrin Dungey. "I had a lot of ideas in that vein. But J. J. felt it'd be better to keep things as they were, that there would be a beautiful payoff if Francie was the anchor in Sydney's life."

**Sydney and Marshall share a moment at SD-6. "I think this is the 'Everybody Loves Sydney' show," Weisman laughs. "Every man who comes across her path is enamored of her, and rightfully so. I think Marshall has a little bit of a crush on her. He gets nervous around everybody, and especially nervous around her because of her beauty and grace."**

"Early on, we had discussions with Ron about his character to understand Sloane's madness, his psychopathy," Ken Olin recalled. "There was an episode I directed where Sloane distrusts Sydney and has her brought to him. Sloane tells her that he knew her parents, that he's known her since she was a child. At that point we began to get into his emotional stakes in regards to Sydney. We weren't any longer seeing him as just the antagonist who runs SD-6, but seeing this part of him that has a very perverted relationship to her, a kind of twisted love."

In episode 18, "Masquerade," Sydney goes to Sloane and asks him for help in finding her mother. Sloane initially refuses, citing her duty to SD-6, but then—suddenly—he changes, sitting close to Sydney, gently touching her as he looks deeply into her eyes and says that, yes, he'll help her. When the *Alias* cast went to work the Monday after that episode aired, Garner gave Rifkin some feedback on that scene.

"We were on location and I'd just finished my scene," Rifkin recalled, "and as I was passing Jennifer, who was going to do her scene, she said to me, 'Wasn't that creepy, our scene last night?' Jennifer said her mother had called her and said, 'Tell Ron we love him, but we didn't like the way he was touching you; it was very weird.' I did a part, this character

Julian Fisher, on *Sex and the City* with Sarah [Jessica Parker], who is a close friend, but watching me come on to her on screen freaked me out. That's how I felt with Jennifer, because we're such good friends and it was creepy. I choose to think that it means that Sloane loves her as a father—that's as far as I'll go with this. If it turns out to be something else, it'll really freak me out!

"I actually don't think of Sloane as a villain," Rifkin added. "I can't approach him as a villain. I have to play it as if I'm a guy who has principles and morals. The fact that he has to do some bad things, well, we may find out that the people he had to do away with were really KGB or whatever. I've played some heavies, but I have a personal side that's generally warm and friendly, so I think J.J. cast against type. But I think that was actually important for this character because there's confusion in this show, the relationships are all askew."

For Will Tippin, Sydney was the love that got away. But not even this kiss can stir Sydney to be more than just friends.

It's not all grim reality inside SD-6. There's the normal bustle and energy of a busy office, with genuinely likable figures like agent Dixon. And an indispensable part of every SD-6 strategy session is Marshall, a character actor Kevin Weisman notes is a "shout out" to Desmond Llewelyn, the late actor who played Q, the gadget master who kept James Bond accessorized. "But I didn't pattern my character after that actor," Weisman added. "We've also taken that classic 'mission' scenario and added our own *Alias* twist."

Although the script is the Word at *Alias*, Weisman could stay true to the "specific computer jargon" portions of the script while having the freedom to spontaneously break into Marshall-esque tangents. "Originally, as it was written in the pilot, Marshall was very much about the facts, so

**Sydney at the bedside of Agent Dixon, who's recovering from nearly fatal gunshot wounds suffered during a battle at Mount Aconcagua for possession of the prized Rambaldi manuscript. One of Sydney's internal conflicts is that as a double agent she's betraying her partner, who mistakenly believes that SD-6 really is a covert arm of the CIA.**

we had to create that tangent and funny stuff," Weisman recalled. "They gracefully and graciously let me run my mouth, to do my own thing, and if it worked, it ended up on Sunday night. But I didn't have to do as much improvisation as the season went on because the writers locked in to my Marshall mannerisms and speech patterns and they wrote some really funny stuff and solid tangents."

A major series premise—that most of the patriotic American agents of SD-6 don't realize they're working for the "other side"—posed a constant challenge for the creators, Alexander admitted. "Dixon has been a challenge. I mean, his partner is doing all this stuff [CIA countermissions] under his nose, and how do you do that every week without making the guy seem like an idiot? So, in episode five ["Doppelgänger"] we had Sydney secretly deactivate a bomb, to foil the SD-6 mission to blow up a plant. But Dixon, because he's a smart guy, has brought along a secondary detonator and he blows it up, he's successful in the mission. But it's killed some CIA agents who were secretly in the plant. For Sydney it's a disaster."

Sydney Bristow displays her fighting skills. In designing such fight sequences, fight coordinator David Morizot works out the moves by talking to the writers and the episode director, and doing a "walk-through" with Garner's stunt double, Shauna Duggins. Morizot explains, "I picture it all in my head. I like each move to flow like water. Once we have it down, I'll present it to J.J. and the episode director. Then, hopefully, we have time to rehearse!"

Sydney looks fashionable while fighting Anna Espinosa (Gina Torres), her foe from the rival spy agency, K-Directorate. Sydney's fighting spirit was summed up in a first-season thank-you letter that Morizot gave the cast and crew: "[I]f you're ever in a tight situation in your life, just remember to ask yourself, 'How would Sydney handle this?'"

Carl Lumbly reasoned that Sydney has withheld the truth from Dixon because of her fiancé's death, that shattering lesson about what happens when one betrays SD-6, and also because she can't predict Dixon's reaction. In Lumbly's view, his character's not knowing about his partner's betrayal was no different from a spouse who's unaware of a cheating partner—sometimes the evidence is all around but the betrayed, in his trust, can't see it. Indeed, Dixon has convinced his own beloved wife that he's an investment banker at Credit Dauphine.

Dixon's story line took a dramatic turn at the end of the season as he not only became suspicious that Sydney was a traitor, but confronted her about his concerns. "I think each actor handles a character differently," Lumbly reflected. "At the end of the day, I can definitely walk away from my character. But I've noticed I'm more observant, because that's the function of these [secret agent] people. For them, unfortunately, it's an awareness of potential danger. I might be driving and I'll see a guy trying to jimmy his car door. I don't make a citizen's arrest, but I'm thinking, 'Maybe he's forgotten his keys.' I practice what Dixon's life must involve, which is being aware and alert.

"When I started this role, I wanted to find out more about the intelligence community. I read about the Book of Honor that lists all the fallen heroes of the CIA. But not all the fallen heroes can be in the book because many operations remain classified and the relatives of agents killed in those operations may not know how they died. The cover stories are still in place, like a family being told an individual died in an automobile accident in Tunisia while in actuality it was a plane crash in Kenya. That kind of research sticks in places, so when we get into these fictitious situations I have something to reference. It gives you fake memories, I guess."

# INSIDE THE CIA

In the real world, the Central Intelligence Agency has a problematic past. Back in the Camelot days of the Kennedy administration the agency was developing a program of "executive action," code words for the political assassination unit that went under the name ZR/Rifle. The unit's exotic gadgets included a poison syringe in the form of a fountain pen, an assassination device planned for Cuban leader Fidel Castro. On the other side of that coin are undeniable national security needs and even such applauded operations as the agency's little-known efforts in the 1950s and '60s to aid Tibetan resistance against the invading Chinese.

J. J. Abrams could have developed a fictitious intelligence agency to represent America but decided to present a glorified CIA. "Since *The X-Files* is prototypical of an evil government agency show in the audience's mind, I thought, Why not let them [a government agency] be the good guys?" Abrams recalled. "I loved the idea that the CIA would be on Sydney's side and that she was this patriotic young woman who was the one person trying to take control of this impossible situation."

While crafting the screenplay for the pilot, Abrams realized that there might be another story line on the CIA side—Sydney's handler, Agent Vaughn, could be a potential love interest. Abrams had been scripting the scene of their first meeting, with Sydney having boldly marched into CIA headquarters to write down everything she knew about SD-6, when he realized Sydney's handler could be so much more. "Their potential love interest hadn't occurred to me as I was writing their first scene together. That scene was going to be the set-up for the next scene, where Sydney's at a cemetery and her father shows up and tells her that she's in, she's been accepted as a double agent for the CIA. But I sort of stumbled upon it—it was, 'Oh, my God!' It became clear to me in that scene, as Vaughn looks at Sydney while she's writing her statement, that he finds her attractive. From there it became obvious that Vaughn and Sydney would have a relationship."

The other layer of complexity was that agency protocol dictated that Sydney and Vaughn be professionals—there's no office romance between agent and handler. As such, their obvious attraction would have the flavor of the forbidden fruit. "In this day and age, when there are no limits, it's almost impossible to find that sort of modern Victorian romance where the lovers can't be together," Abrams noted.

"I think my character is a pretty straightforward guy who likes his job," Vartan added. "Then this woman comes in and rocks his world and he's struggling with those feelings and trying not to let them interfere as he tries to do his job. My character's romantic struggle is actually similar to who I am. I don't get too emotional about relationships—you either like each other and it works or you don't and it doesn't work. My character doesn't think he can ever be with Sydney unless she's no longer working [as an agent]. That's easy to play, those are really broad strokes—I like her; can't be with her."

*Alias* **is full of worlds within worlds, and nothing is as it seems. Even mighty SD-6 is part of a larger pic-ture—over it is the umbrella of evil known as the Alliance. The heads of the Alliance's twelve cells are convened here.**

# SECRETS

One of the "third layer" aspects of *Alias* is that virtually all the main char-acters have a secret side or hidden agenda. Even Francie, the most removed from the intrigues swirling around Sydney Bristow, in one episode engaged Sydney's help to spy on her boyfriend. That web of deceit in which all the characters were entangled got even stickier throughout the season as the big question was asked: What comes next? Bradley Cooper noted that he'd once overheard some of the production crew—hardy veterans who'd seen it all—asking if anyone had seen the latest script, wondering what was next.

Sometimes, insider knowledge was apportioned to the actors by J. J. Abrams when that insight was needed to inform a performance. "There were a few points where I had trouble in terms of understanding how to play a certain thing and I had to go to J.J. so I could understand how to play it, and he was very helpful," Ron Rifkin recalled. "I'd never done anything like this before. Usually you have a more complete sense of your character. I'm from the theater, where we have a sense of a beginning, a middle, and an end. As the season unfolded, certainly for my character, I found out more about him—it was an adventure. Oddly, it didn't seem to get in the way, the not knowing, at least for me. There are people who think I might be Sydney's father, others don't know if I'm supposed to be good or bad. That's the nature of this show, it's filled with so many dichotomies and points of view."

A major surprise was that Laura Bristow might be alive. At one point, Abrams clued Garber in on that impending revelation. "I didn't know at the beginning of the season, but it was very helpful when it was revealed to me that she married [Jack] to get information. It helped me to give Jack a level of despair and sadness that was even deeper than what I'd been exploring. This guy is operating from a place of pain and that information fed that.

"But what's fun about doing this show, particularly one as well written as this one, is that everything unfolds, things are revealed. Just as in real life, tragedy or good fortune can strike at unexpected times and that's what happens every week on *Alias*."

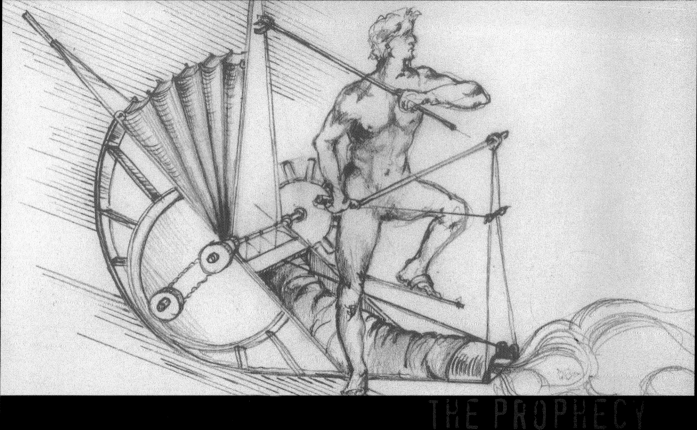

THE PROPHECY

Milo Rambaldi would doubtless appreciate that his legend, forged in the Renaissance, was being detailed on *Alias* Internet sites in the twenty-first century. Rambaldi was born in Parma in 1444 and died a lonely man, without spouse or heirs, in the winter of 1496. Toward the end of his life, Rambaldi enjoyed a meteoric rise to power upon being privately retained as "architect, consultant, and prophet" to Cardinal Alexander when he became Pope in 1492.

But the prophet's declaration that one day science would allow human beings to know God was considered rank heresy, and Rambaldi was excommunicated from the Church the year of his death. Powerful enemies, led by Archdeacon Claudio Vespertini, sought to keep Rambaldi's theories contained and eventually expunged his name from all public monuments and destroyed his workshops.

Will, Francie, and Sydney on a rare night out. The fun will be short-lived—Ms. Bristow is about to be taken away by government agents for questioning regarding the Rambaldi Prophecy.

But Rambaldi's works survived, from secret laboratories uncovered soon after his death to the puzzle pieces of the prophet's artifacts, many of them inscribed with his mystic symbol and layered with

Jack Bristow and Agent Vaughn spring Sydney from her FBI captors so she can disprove her alleged connection to the Rambaldi Prophecy.

inscriptions and secret codes. Rambaldi's papers reveal that he had developed both a prototype of the twentieth-century transistor and a "machine code" language. Most chilling of the deciphered codes of Rambaldi was his apocalyptic Prophecy. According to one page of this recovered manuscript, a woman would fulfill the Prophecy.

In modern times, Rambaldi's reputation was darkened by the fascination he held for Adolf Hitler during the Third Reich's global search for talismans and secrets of occult power. The Führer reportedly had his own code word for Rambaldi: "Nostravinci."

# RAMBALDI: THE TRUTH

There are kernels of truth in the Rambaldi legend, including the existence of a historical Pope Alexander VI. And Adolf Hitler did seek out objects of occult power, sending Nazi research expeditions to remote areas of mystic Tibet.

But the real truth about Rambaldi is he's a total fabrication of J. J. Abrams and his writers—the very name is inspired by Carlo Rambaldi, the effects artist who designed E.T., the extraterrestrial of movie fame. And Nostravinci wasn't Hitler's appellation for the prophet and seer but *Alias* writers'-room shorthand for a character imagined as a composite of Nostradamus and Leonardo da Vinci. "Figuring out the questions about

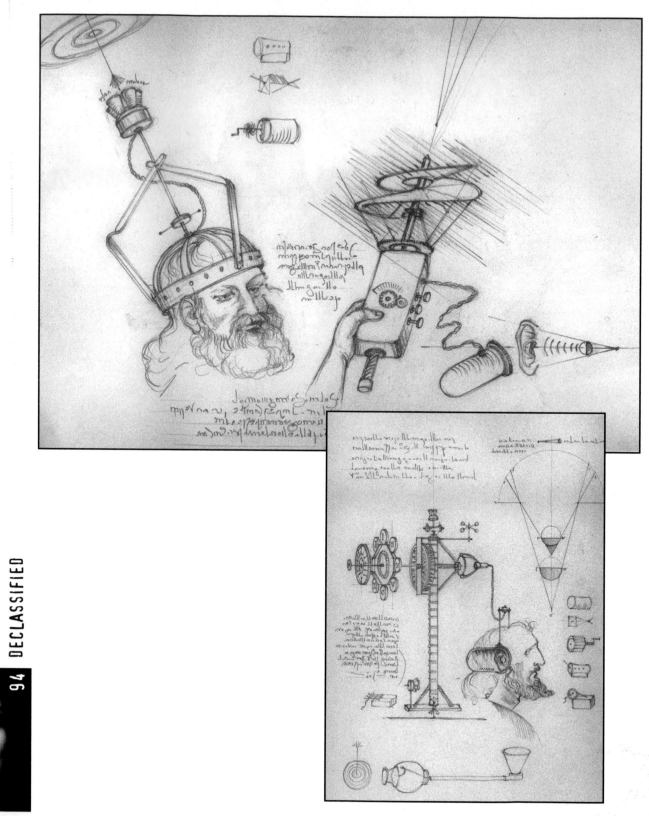

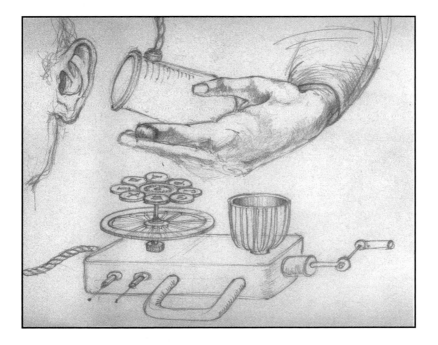

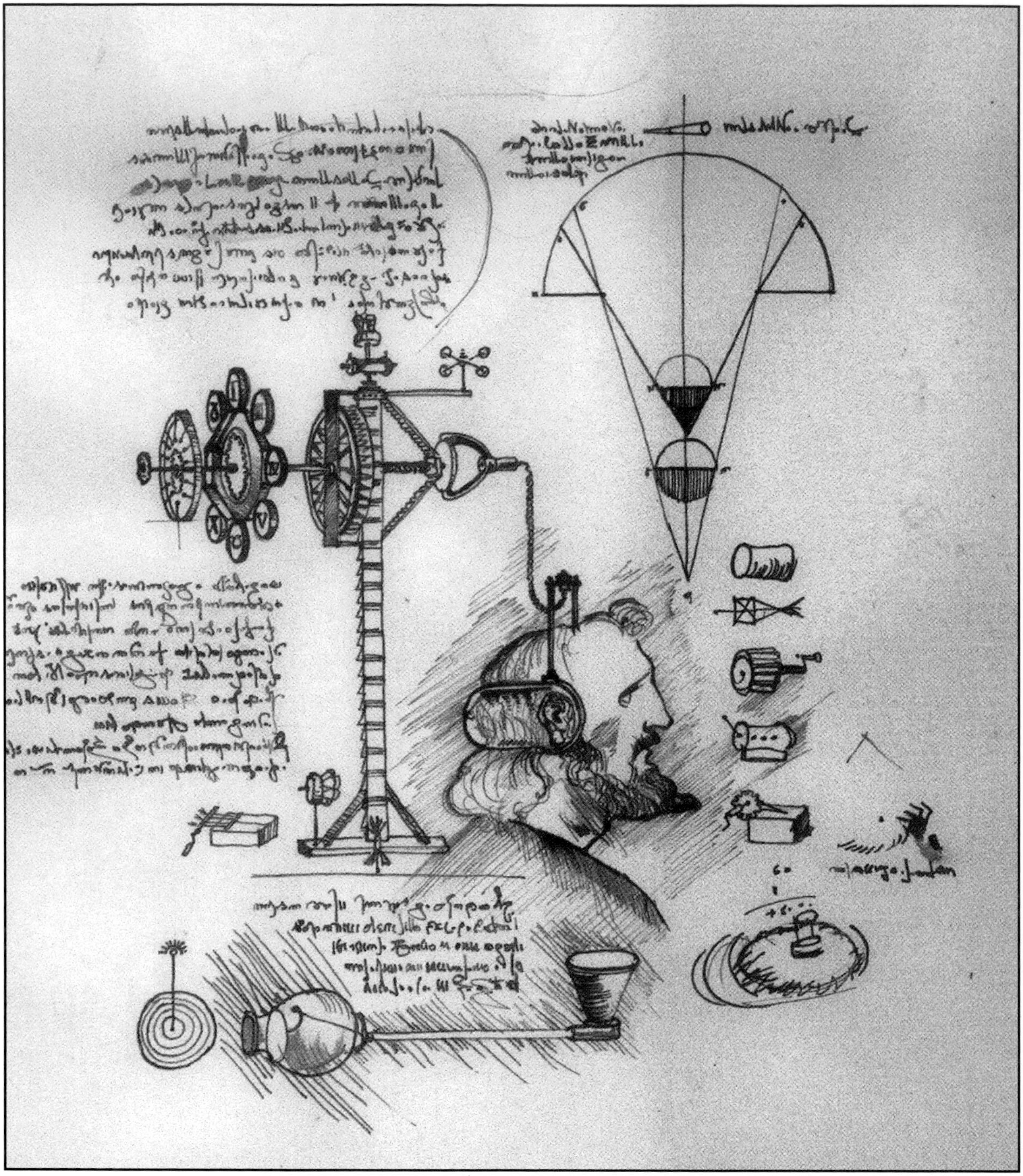

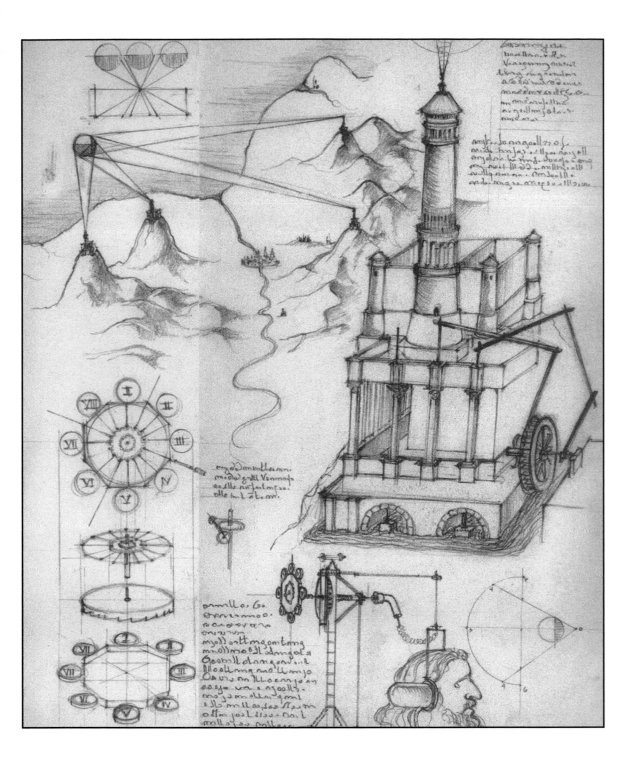

Rambaldi—who he was and what he did—I got a crash course in the 1500s," *Alias* technical consultant Rick Orci said with a grin, explaining that Rambaldi was inspired by bits and pieces of historical truths. "Pope Alexander VI was alive in that time. It was also a period when popes commissioned architects to build elaborate things. We built on that."

In the grand plan of *Alias* the Rambaldi mystery is an integral and ongoing story line that, Abrams promised, will be explored in greater depth in the show's second season. "For me [the Rambaldi story] ratchets up the uniqueness of *Alias*. The show is not just about spies and going after nuclear codes or whatever—it's about something weirder."

## THE RAMBALDI DEBATE

Toward the end of the first season the writers began contemplating story lines for the next season. Roberto Orci observed that the Rambaldi story is the biggest debate.

"Something like the Charlie character isn't as high stakes, but the Prophecy, where you set up a high degree of expectation, can turn off a lot of people if it's done wrong," Roberto mused. "The Prophecy could determine whether *Alias* is a world where things like ghosts might exist. It could suddenly put everything in the wrong focus."

Abrams revealed one final Rambaldi tidbit for this dossier: "In the opening title, right before *Alias* flashes on the screen, there's a hidden sign of Rambaldi in one of the frames. I put the symbol in the pilot and it's still there."

THE MISSIONS: LIVE ACTION

Technical advisor Rick Orci was a major touchstone for ensuring that even the most fantastic story point was plausible, from the feasibility of a Marshall gadget to a piece of historical data. "I'm usually in the writers' room with the writers to help brainstorm the story, and then I'll help the writer who writes the script," Rick explained. "If it's a plot point about,

**Agent Vaughn officiates at a CIA ceremony for agents who have paid the ultimate price. It's a poignant moment for Sydney's handler—his own father was an intelligence officer killed in the line of duty.**

say, decrypting a satellite communications system, I have to research that. I don't call anybody but usually find it myself. It's ridiculous how much information is on the Internet, you can literally punch something up almost instantly."

Rick explained that a paranormal research arm of the National Security Agency, the Department of Special Research (DSR), which came into *Alias* on the wave of the Rambaldi Prophecy story line, paralleled the CIA's own Office of Scientific Intelligence, which dealt with remote viewing and other paranormal phenomenon. And while the brainwashed and programmed SD-6 assassin Martin Shepard recalled the main

**Sydney is committed to a Bucharest mental institution to gain the confidence of mentally ill Martin Shepard (John Hannah), a secret assassin with information SD-6 desires.**

character in the classic Cold War–era film *The Manchurian Candidate*, the inspiration for his creation was actually a CIA plan from the 1950s.

A guiding point for the *Alias* writers was that the CIA cannot by law operate inside the United States. "You can't have the CIA just arresting people [in the U.S.], so that's where we'll bring in other agencies, to maintain reality," Rick explained. "In 'The Box,' Agent Vaughn storms SD-6, which he really can't do, because he's on U.S. soil. I think everybody [the writers] knew that, everyone here is so smart it makes my job easier. So we fudged that by showing that he did it without authorization and got in trouble for it, and, secondly, that with the USA PATRIOT Act passed after 9-11 the CIA had been given the benefit of the doubt in certain situations."

During the first season, Rick Orci even created an internal Web site for the writers that was filled with his research

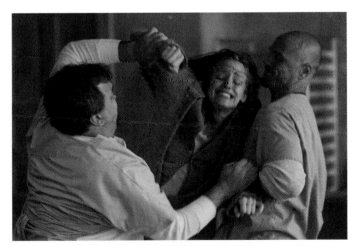

**Sydney has trouble gaining Shepard's trust and discovers that the hospital is a K-Directorate front. When she finally escapes with Shepard, the programmed assassin's memory returns—and with it the revelation that he was the assassin who killed Sydney's fiancé. That shattering flashback was staged as a long Steadicam shot by stunt coordinator and second unit director Jeff Habberstad.**

Sydney and Vaughn contemplate the deadly, "fail-safe" explosive charges they must disarm before McKenas Cole opens the SD-6 vault in "The Box." "I defy anyone not to have chemistry with her," Michael Vartan says of Jennifer Garner. "I don't know what it's called, you can't buy it or earn it, you've got it or you don't—and she's got it. When you're acting with her, and I've heard this from the other cast members, you get energized."

on intelligence agencies, weapons and communications systems, and cutting-edge technology from around the world. "Everything on the site is categorized so the writers can do the research themselves," Orci explained. "If Sydney is going to a certain country, and they want to know what intelligence agencies are there, they can go get that profile. I keep adding to the Web site—it grows and grows."

# THE NATURAL

Jeff Habberstad, *Alias* stunt coordinator and second unit director, came to the show starting with the first regular-season episode, "So It Begins." A veteran movie stunt coordinator expert at wire rigs for "flying" performers (one of his recent features was the 2002 release *Spider-Man*), Habberstad had never worked as a production principal on television before joining *Alias*. "To be honest, I'm pretty successful working in features, so I was skeptical about doing a TV show," Habberstad said. "But they [the production] wanted a feature look to the show and my skepticism went away."

Stunts usually require that harnesses and attached wires be hidden (or digitally erased), but an *Alias* advantage was that harnesses and wires can be another piece of equipment in the secret agent's kit bag. The advantages of on-camera harnesses aside, Garner's stunt assignments were daunting, even for a trained stuntperson. Habberstad's verdict? "She's a natural."

Garner's first work for Habberstad was a scene of Sydney stepping off the top of an elevator into the shaft, a stunt which dropped her twenty-five feet on a wire harness. "That twenty-five-foot fall was like falling off a two-and-a-half-story building—it started from there," Habberstad said.

In episode 9, "Mea Culpa," Garner made one of the most dramatic entrances of the series, a parachute drop into a nighttime party scene. The stunt, staged at a mansion at Griffith Park in Los Angeles, dropped Garner one hundred feet in a steerable black parachute that the actress maneuvered to land in front of camera. "That was a real parachute landing on the deck of this mansion, no blue screen," Habberstad noted. "We hoisted her up on a crane with one wire dressed to look like one of the parachute lines. The parachute was spread out and hanging off a spreader bar, a big, square piece of aluminum, so when it caught air it'd work like a real parachute. As soon as we gave the line slack and let her go, the parachute naturally inflated and she floated and steered it to the ground.

When she landed, she ripped off her diving clothes and went from being a skydiver to a beautifully dressed partygoer in about a second and a half."

In the show's early brainstorming days, Habberstad visited the writers' room to lay out possible stunts to consider for the episodes ahead. One of his ideas envisioned Sydney going from building to building on a wire. The writers eventually wrote that stunt into a mission to Moscow for episode 14, "The Coup," wherein Sydney crosses buildings on a wire to a top-floor window to observe a fateful meeting between the head of the K-Directorate spy agency and Mr. Sark, a representative of The Man. But the scripted stunt set off alarm bells in the offices of Touchstone and ABC.

"When Jennifer was going to climb building to building on a wire almost a hundred feet above the ground—that got everyone's attention," Habberstad recalled. "At first they said she couldn't do it, but we reassured everyone Jennifer would be safe. I explained the mechanics and engineering to put everyone at ease. She was going to be on a harness hooked onto a Spectra line, a blend of nylon and other cords. It's a thirty-thousand-pound line, size for size it's stronger than steel cable. When you put a single person on that, it puts things in perspective. Just looking at her a hundred feet above ground made for a real impressive shot."

Garner's action-hero persona was also built on Sydney's trademark fight scenes. While fight coordinator David Morizot worked with the actress on blocking out those action sequences, costumer Laura Goldsmith often had to provide fashionable, yet functional, outfits. Late in the season, such an outfit was required for a fight in a cabaret (episode 21, "Rendezvous"). "The script called for a sexy dress to go with this big fight scene," Goldsmith recalled. "I think Jennifer was a little worried about it—it was the first time she called me and asked what we were going to do about this outfit. She'd had time to block out this fight in advance, working with the second-unit stuntpeople, and she felt like it was going to be the mother of all fights. There are so many things to consider [in a costume], making something look killer but also being practical in terms of multiples and what you can do in a limited amount of time.

"I decided to go with a beautiful men's-style Armani tuxedo with an amazing corset I got from a store called Agent Provocateur, with a necklace with twenty strands of jet-black beads—it was a cross between *Moulin Rouge* and *Cabaret*. It was sexy and elegant, yet functional for the fight scene. She was also in high heels, which we switched out for a flat heel during the main shooting. I had one outfit for her and her stuntperson and three or four multiples in case something got ripped."

*Alias* special effects coordinator John Downey, a veteran of film work from recent Arnold Schwarzenegger films to *Men in Black II*, echoed Habberstad's assessment of the trust Garner placed in the various teams

Sydney and fellow SD-6 agent—and former lover—Noah Hicks pose as hikers to gain access to a secret Alexander Khasinau facility. After the mission, the two agents spend a romantic night at an SD-6 safe house. "We actually had gotten a letter we kept for a while in the writers' room from a woman who said Sydney was such a great role model and to make sure she didn't have sex with anybody," says Jesse Alexander. "I'm sorry we had to disappoint her."

that helped her with the physical side of her character. "She's comfortable with us because we don't try to sneak anything past her," Downey noted. "She's aware of what's going on."

Downey (who alternated special effects duties throughout the season with Bruce Kuroyama) recalled that one dangerous stunt was staged at night at an old Nike missile site northwest of the San Fernando Valley, which stood in for the island of Crete in episode 11, "The Confession." Filming in an actual bunker, Downey affixed a sprinkler system to a water truck to create the illusion of the spray of gasoline that drenches the room. In the story, Sydney escapes just as a spark ignites the gasoline-soaked bunker, an effect that had Garner running past fireballs fired from propane cannons. Camera angles made the explosions seem closer than they were. "We had propane mortars, which are like beer kegs with a quick-release valve, and you build up the pressure to make a bigger fireball—we electronically set off three of those behind her," Downey said. "Propane fire is fairly safe and cool, if there is such a thing, as opposed to a gasoline fire."

As Sydney's double-agent father, Victor Garber also got in on the action-hero act. Whether staring down Hassan's bully boys during a knuckle-sandwich session or returning fire in a pitched gun battle, Jack was every inch the lifelong secret agent. Looking back on the first season, Garber singled out "the Cuba episode" as one of his favorites. That episode (episode 10, "Spirit"), was Jack's first real mission in the series. He had to stay stoic through a battering at the hands of arms dealer Hassan's thugs, keep cool when Hassan orders him to kill a captured Sydney, and finally kidnap the arms dealer for the CIA.

In *Alias* the very locations are aliases, with many Los Angeles–area sites transformed into seemingly foreign locales by Scott Chambliss's department. This view of the abandoned Ambassador Hotel became the Havana compound of arms dealer Ineni Hassan for episode 10, "Spirit."

"I haven't done any [action roles] before *Alias*," Garber said with a laugh. "There were some car maneuvers and gun things in the pilot, but that side of my character was all in J.J.'s head and it evolved as it went along. After my character's first mission to Cuba, I said, 'No more missions, Daddy's tired.' But later, I was ready to do more. That physical side of my character surprises me, frankly. I honestly don't know I'll be able to do these things when I read them in the script. Often, you don't know how you'll do it, but that you'll get there—and then you take that leap."

# RESURRECTION

One of the dramatic action sequences—and a turning point in the series mythology—came in "Q & A" when Sydney is sprung from her FBI interrogators by her father and Vaughn so she can be free to disprove the dreaded Rambaldi Prophecy. Pesky CIA agent Haladki learns of Sydney's escape and sounds the alarm, and soon a fleet of squad cars are chasing Sydney's car, finally cornering her at a pier. Sydney waits as the tension-packed seconds tick by, her car's engine idling, the police officers out with guns aimed, calling for her to surrender.

"I designed those shots because, to me, the whole episode shifts in that moment—what is she thinking, what's she feeling here?" episode director Ken Olin recalled. "We've gone from this wild car chase to this psychological and emotional moment." Sydney slams on the accelerator and drives off the pier. She survives by breathing air from the tire valve and slipping away under cover of night.

**Some L.A.–area locations were exotic to begin with, such as a private ranch in Malibu that became Denpassar in episode 20. "There was this fantastic, crazy place that looked Indonesian," Chambliss says. "We turned that into a thoroughfare and a private palace."**

In breaking down the dramatic action sequence, a number of events had to be choreographed, including the car chase (filmed on a Saturday in the coastal town of San Pedro near the relatively deserted dock area) and the live action of Sydney's car going off the pier (complete with breakaway fencing made out of balsa wood). These scenes would cut with the scenes of the submerged car filmed the day before at an outdoor water tank at Universal Studios.

The logistics, as coordinated by producer Sarah Caplan, began with checking local river depths. Because the water level was dangerously low, the originally scripted idea of Sydney driving off a bridge into a river (duplicating Laura Bristow's fateful "accident") was changed to Sydney driving off a pier into the ocean. The car chase and dock work at the San Pedro docks were scheduled, the Universal water tank reserved.

Sydney's car itself, which had to come in multiples for several special effects takes, had to match the car in a "live" TV version of the police pursuit Will and Francie are watching at home—in reality, stock footage of an actual car chase. The kicker was that Caplan had to put all the logistics in motion—within four days.

Downey called the "Q & A" car work "the biggest thing I've done on this show. We launched two cars into the ocean in one day, something that'd normally take two guys four days to prep and two days to shoot. The production's transportation department got us the cars and we were prepping while they were painting, everybody sort of dog-piled on it. We had to 'EPA it,' meaning anything you put into a body of water you have to pull out the engine and transmission, clean out the oil and brake fluid. One of the cars we put in the ocean was actually a car we ended up putting into the water tank at Universal."

For the water tank stunt, an entire gutted car—with Jennifer Garner inside—was raised and lowered by a twenty-five-ton crane to the bottom of the tank. All the windows were rolled up and extra holes punched into the floor to allow water to flow in quickly. There were safety divers at the bottom and a scuba tank hidden in the car, but Garner still had to wait until the car filled with water before being able to roll down the window and make her escape.

"The first take, you could tell she wasn't doing much acting—it was all concern on her face," Downey said. "Luckily, she's comfortable in the water. After she got out through the window she could then breathe oxygen from the valve stem of one of the tires. We'd rigged the tire with a real valve stem and gutted it out and ran a hose out the back side. One of our guys was down in the water and when it looked like she was breathing, he'd push on a valve and it'd send air out so she could actually breathe out of it."

"The first take was freaky," Garner recalled. "What was scary was it was mental. I had to sit very calmly, buckled up in the car, as it completely filled up with water, and if you take your last breath too early and run out of oxygen you're almost hyperventilating because you're freaking out. But once the first take was over, I loved the rest of the day. It was like being a fish in the water."

That watery death trap could have been the typical cliffhanger scenario, but the episode actually ended on a more chilling note—Sydney's realization that her mother might have similarly survived her own watery car crash. Director Olin noted that the final scene, between Sydney and her father, was one of the toughest aspects of the episode, staged as it was only three hours after the stunt car had been shot off the San Pedro pier. "The hardest part of the ambitions of this show, from a production point of view, is switching gears, as in going from filming this huge action sequence to Jennifer having to go to a place [inside herself] where she has to convey these powerful emotions. She's devastated as she meets her father to say, 'I think my mother is alive.' "

# LOCATION WORK

In the first season all the distant locations visited each week—from Hong Kong and Cairo to Moscow and Paris—were conjured. Only once did the production venture outside greater Los Angeles, taking a hop to Las Vegas for a weekend shoot for episode 14, "The Coup." "My dad still doesn't believe we haven't gone to Paris or Hong Kong," Jesse Alexander said, laughing. "We rarely leave Burbank, but people believe we've been all these places. It's amazing."

Creating those distant places often required digital visual effects. But often, nearby places were simply transformed. In the *Alias* writers' room are huge books filled with photographs, the results of Los Angeles–area

location scouts Sarah Caplan's department undertook in the show's very early days, with production designer Chambliss's department also providing location research photos. While some scouted areas were suitable for settings in the show's Los Angeles milieu, the bolder ambition was for scouted locations that could stand in for far-flung places.

For example, Caplan (who likes to keep many of her prized location finds secret) discovered a decaying old mausoleum with distinctly Arabic architecture—a spot ultimately transformed into a Moroccan marketplace for episode 4, "A Broken Heart." At that locale, as with every other location venue, the key to transformation was camera position and composition and Scott Chambliss's design approach and set dressing.

The actual episode prep work often involved DP Bonvillain sending lighting tech John Smith and key grip Duane Journey to scout a specific location and take video and photos that would be discussed with production designer Scott Chambliss. Such production teamwork transformed the Ambassador Hotel in Los Angeles into the Havana compound of arms dealer Hassan.

The hotel, where Senator Robert Kennedy was assassinated in 1968, had been abandoned for years. "It's a rambling, grand old place with a huge lobby that's gone to seed—it really looked like Cuba for that episode," said Bonvillain, who credited the location with providing about 70 percent of the convincing illusion, while camera filters and bright lights gave the conjured Cuba a warm, golden hue. "Every element of Sydney's life has a special look—SD-6 is a dangerous place, so we light it with a cool, bluish color while the CIA is more drab and colorless—and when she goes on a mission we want to light it so it'll look like a different place. It seemed right to make Cuba look warmer."

The most astounding aspect of transforming a local landmark into a foreign locale was not merely the realism of the final illusion but the speed with which it was created. "Even in the best of circumstances we had only seven or eight days to prep a location, and by the end of the season we were down to one," Chambliss explained. "In the beginning, when we had more prep time, we'd pull out the location photo research books or go to the location with the director to talk about the things that could happen there, and then pencils would start going onto paper. But at the end of the season it was like we were always shot out of a cannon—we knew what to do."

Of course, no location could beat those closest to the production's home base—the Disney lot itself. "Location" work outside the soundstage walls took place everywhere from the ABC building to the underground tunnels Disney built during the classic years of animation (which allowed celluloid art to be taken from the Animation Building to the Ink and Paint Building without being ruined by bad weather).

Jack Bristow, battered but indomitable, during McKenas Cole's siege of SD-6.

Jack helps CIA agent Paul Kelvin (Tom Everett) maintain his cover as German scientist Jeroen Schiller—breaking his arm in the process. "Victor's character is so introverted, but when the action starts he explodes," says fight coordinator David Morizot. "Victor had a really good fight in a café against three or four guys in the Cuba episode. Initially, he was nervous about whether he could pull it off. But he certainly pulled it off. He was 'Action Man' that day."

"Towards the end of the season someone made a joke that a certain episode would mark the last unphotographed place on the lot," Caplan said, smiling. "But soon after that we were scouting the lot—and we found a whole new set of corridors! It was, 'Oh, my God, this is great!' It was remarkable because, believe me, we scoured this lot."

Vaughn and Sydney race down a hallway as a bomb explodes and turns the Muller device into water in the season finale.

**The Prophecy**

Scene F7 - Woods - Night

Shot # 4

Lo - Angle

CAM. Pulls BACK AS SHE RUNS

SQUIB HIT

Shot # 5

The killer dogs are pursuing Sydney Bristow and her fear is palpable as she sprints through rugged terrain to a deadly precipice. She takes a seemingly suicidal leap—but her fall is arrested as a parachute built into her backpack billows open and she gently drifts across a glorious golden sky above Rio. It's one of Sydney's more dramatic cliffhanger escapes—and a total illusion.

When a shot needed something more than set dressing and props to conjure some distant locale—anything from recognizable landmarks to entire background skylines—that shot went to visual effects supervisor Kevin Blank. Throughout the season, Blank delegated shots to a freelance squad

**"The idea from the start was to sell these distant locations without going around the world,"** says visual effects supervisor Kevin Blank. Above is one of the first season's trademark visual effects shots, a panoramic image of Rio.

of visual effects artists (including Eric Chauvin and his Blackpool Studios, Bill Mather of Mather Art, and Bob Lloyd's Fuzzy Logic Productions) and coordinated production with J. J. Abrams and Sarah Caplan (on creative and cost issues, respectively), writers, episode directors, DP Michael Bonvillain, and, as in the case of the Rio shot, stunt coordinator Jeff Habberstad.

The Rio escape provides a textbook example of crafting visual effects in the digital age. The "live-action" footage was staged at the Disney Ranch in Southern California, where Habberstad's crew lifted Garner up on a fifty-foot scissors lift for a dive into a stunt pad. To facilitate the illusion of Sydney leaping off the precipice, the pad was covered in greenscreen, a green colored backing material that allows effects artists to digitally composite in another image. In this case, the neutral greenscreen background was replaced with digitally painted trees and rocky foreground and the final image composited with computer-scanned footage of Sydney making her leap.

"One of the scariest stunts I did all year was parachuting into that greenscreen," Garner added. "They've dropped me from a hundred feet up, but it's one thing to be dropped, where you have no control and you're along for the ride, and another thing to leap off a platform—into nothing. It wasn't dangerous, I was on a wire that caught me [before hitting the pad]. It's just a mental thing, your body doesn't want to do that. But when you do it once you're fine."

The expansive final shot of the double agent floating over a golden tableau of Rio was completely conjured, from the computer-generated stuntperson to the digitally processed photographic view of the city. "We call our computer-generated stuntpeople puppets," Blank said of the shot's three-dimensional animated figure. "We'd actually filmed an element of Jennifer turning on a greenscreen, which we were going to reduce down and add a parachute in 3-D, but we decided it didn't look exciting enough. So we built a 3-D version of Jennifer. We could get a more dynamic camera move as we animated the 3-D puppet, with realistic motion blur, through a background that is essentially a still photograph."

That high-resolution photo of Rio was digitized and seamlessly composited with the 3-D animation using After Effects, a commercial software program. The final image was further embellished with painted elements of background mountains and the sky as well as lighting highlights and even a photographic lens flare element.

The live-action greenscreen stunt of Sydney Bristow parachuting off a cliff in Rio originally envisioned a hang glider popping out of Sydney's backpack. "I couldn't see something as big as a hang glider popping out of this tiny backpack," Jeff Habberstad recalls. "J.J. had also pictured it as being a parachute, so somehow the wrong idea had come down the pipes."

The sequence was first plotted out by storyboard artist Tom O'Neill.

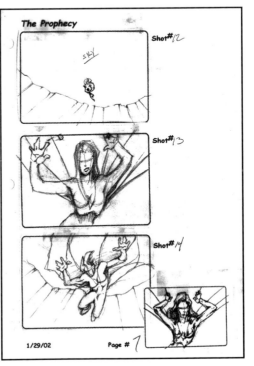

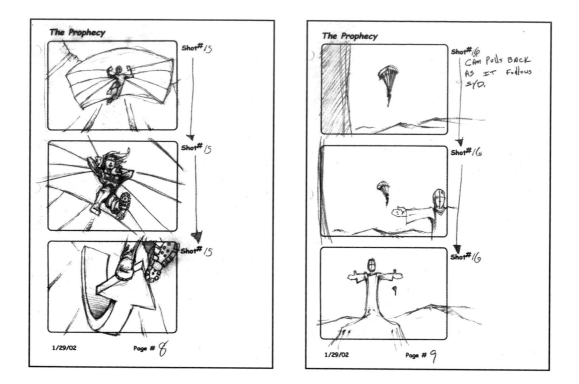

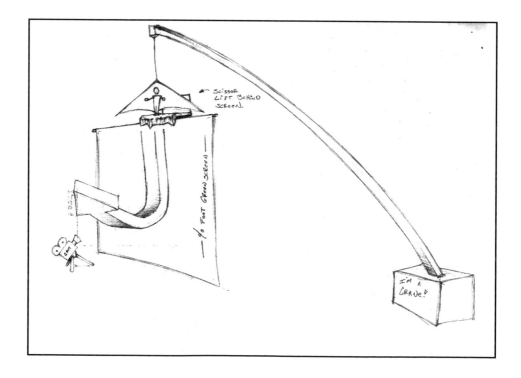

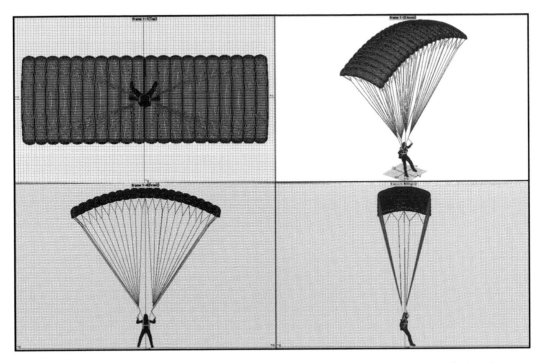

The elements of the final, expansive view of Sydney gliding over Rio included a three-dimensional computer-graphics parachute model, which was first built as a 3-D wireframe. Photography of the real, stunt parachute was then digitally applied—or "texture mapped"—to the wireframe.

The image of Sydney Bristow was a CGI (computer graphic imagery) model—a "puppet" in *Alias* production-speak.

One other touch was added to seal the final Rio shot—color timing to suffuse the scene with a golden glow. "The big stunt sequences for the shot had been filmed from three-thirty to five-thirty in the afternoon, so there was a nice, golden rim light on her," Blank noted. "We asked Michael Bonvillain if we could time the rest of the sequence in that direction and that's what was delivered."

**Final image.**

The "Hong Kong shot" for "The Coup" transformed the ABC building and the adjacent Disney lot in Burbank into a Hong Kong harbor view. In creating the shot, effects artist Eric Chauvin digitally replaced the exterior ABC headquarters logo with "Tyno-Chem Engineering," the corporate front for the FTL spy agency.

# THE HONG KONG SHOT

Visual effects shots are often composite images that integrate scanned photographic elements and digital painting with a real location—the "live plate," as it's called. Such a shot was the dramatic shoot-out scene for "The Coup," set outside a Hong Kong skyscraper in the script—but in reality, in front of the ABC building on Disney's Burbank lot, which was magically transformed with a virtual subway station, background buildings, and even a harbor with a boat cruising past.

For Blank, who prior to *Alias* had spent a year in Hong Kong working on an action film called *Zu Warriors*, the shot was an opportunity to bring to life a great city he knew well. And with a six-week lead time—as opposed to the normal two weeks or less to produce an episode's average slate of ten effects shots—the Hong Kong scene was a rare chance to detail a multi-element, moving-camera effect. "This shot has a higher degree of polish," Blank noted, "because we had more time to tweak it. I know that city in every direction, so I really wanted to go into detail. The produc-

**Chauvin also created a background grid that allowed him to synchronize (or "match move") the location and stock footage camera movements. The resulting composite scene looked like a real shot of Hong Kong filmed with one camera.**

tion wanted to see the Hong Kong skyline, so I went to a stock house and got a moving shot of Hong Kong, not a still photograph. Then we had a camera that was pointed in the direction of the Disney lot and panned to the front of the ABC building. Later, we painted out everything on the Disney lot."

The live-plate part of the shot included an extra walking across the plaza toward the ABC building. The camera tracked the extra to the entrance-way, which erupts in chaos as the head of the FTL spy agency is gunned down by Mr. Sark (played by David Anders), the agent for The Man. The skyline footage, water, and moving boats replaced the Disney lot (which sprawled out opposite the ABC and Feature Animation buildings). The shot began at the subway station that wasn't there, a virtual creation built in the computer using Electric Image modeling software. Blank even contacted a friend in Hong Kong, who went to the actual subway station shown in the stock-footage view to shoot the station's signage. Those details were added to the computer-generated model. (The subway signage work included replacing a subway sign for the Disney/Pixar release *Monsters, Inc.*, which would have dated the episode, and replacing it with signage for *Zu Warriors*.)

The live-action plate with the camera tracking along with the walking man was digitally "match-moved" to the stock footage, so the separately photographed images appeared as if they'd always been a single image shot with one camera. Finally, the ABC logo on the building was digitally replaced with "Tyno-Chem Engineering," the name of the FTL's corporate front.

# THE BIG BROADCAST

Although *Alias* is shot using film, it ends up transferred to the D-5 high-definition format—"the new thing," as Blank described it, noting that high-def for TV was the same high-quality image as so-called high-resolution feature film work. "High-definition masters are the highest format the show exists on," Blank explained. "It's a high-definition cassette that's broadcast simultaneously in standard def and for those who have the separate signal for HD-TV. What's a little frustrating is only about one percent of the population, those with the most expensive TVs and receivers, get the high-definition picture. We do all our effects shots at D-5 resolution, which is about six megabytes per frame as opposed to D-1, which is standard def and about one meg a frame."

The original location photography included trees that Chauvin had to first remove from the footage and then composite back into the image as separate elements, allowing him to control their integration with the new background.

Working in high definition is where budgeted time for effects gets burned, since high-quality images make for bigger files and more number crunching during the compositing and rendering of shots. "I did a few episodes of [the *Star Trek* spin-off] *Enterprise,* and they do effects in standard definition and then up-res to match their final high-definition format," Blank said. "High-def does cost more, and a show like *Enterprise* has a lot more visual effects than we do. But when you up-res, the computer is going through and picking pixels and deciding what is the important information. But that can create problems like artifacting [a defect in the digital image] that has to be fixed later at expense. I think working in low-res is more trouble than it's worth and it's better to just pay the extra money and do it all in high-definition."

POST-PRODUCTION:
PUTTING IT TOGETHER

A young woman's face is submerged in water and she struggles to breathe—the next moment she's thrown to the floor of a dark room by armed guards and strapped into a chair to await her interrogator. She's dressed in black with a bright red wig. Breathing heavily, she knows she's in for hell—and then a quiet, golden-lit university hall appears and this same woman, without the red wig, finishes her essay just as her professor approaches.

Such were the opening scenes of the *Alias* pilot, viewers' first glimpse of Sydney Bristow—by all indications a classic dream sequence. But it became clear that the opening torture scene was real, was actually a vision of the future of this university student, who was a secret agent. On a mission to Taiwan, she would suffer at the hands of the enigmatic figure scripted as Suit and Glasses. Such nonlinear editing was also used in "Q & A;" that episode opened outside the time line with Sydney, disguised in a wig, sitting in her idling car while cornered at the pier.

"If I can tell a fairly simple story in a nonlinear way, it gets my mind going." Abrams smiled. "I love to open with an event that is the linchpin of the whole story, something that you'll catch up to towards the end

"Doing any show you're jumping back and forth from existing in it and seeing it from the outside and trying to figure out how to make it and seeing that everything fits in the bigger picture," says J. J. Abrams. "You're constantly juggling the micro and macro, the practical and the creative." From left to right: Tricia Goken, script supervisor; Michael Bonvillain, director of photography; Brian O. Kelley, 2nd assistant director; and J. J. Abrams.

"Part of the humor of the show is its references to films," reveals Ken Olin. "There might be a scene, say, of betrayal, that's reminiscent of the *Godfather* movies. It's not like the reference itself, but an archetype in any given scene that's based on J.J.'s encyclopedic memory of movies. It's a heightened reality that's part of the show's humor. We love that pop aspect of the show." Pictured left to right: Ken Olin, executive producer; Tom Yatsko, 2nd unit director of photography; Jeff Journey, B camera dolly grip.

of the second act, typically. But when you get to that point in the story, you now understand, but you still have the question—where is this going to go? So, you feel like you've come full-circle but you get the fun of the resolution in the third act."

"There was one episode where I teased J.J. and said, 'I think this is the first time we've ever done a flash forward in a flashback,'" Olin chuckled. "But somehow, that effect does work. J.J. has an extraordinary film vocabulary that allows him to get into the editing room and play with time lines and crosscut between simultaneous action in two different places."

Such decision making happens in the editing room. Unlike the old days of cutting and splicing strips of celluloid, today's editing is accomplished on devices like the Avid, a commercial nonlinear editing machine in which digitized film footage is stored and manipulated.

# EDITING ROOM

While executive producer John Eisendrath focused on breaking a plot and scripting with the writers, Olin was involved in the directing of each episode (both his own work and that of other episode directors) and post-production. Olin explained that the editing process starts with his working a rough cut into shape, then showing it to Abrams. That rough cut can change dramatically, with Abrams and his editors having recourse to all footage.

"J.J. essentially does a lot of rewriting in editing," Olin said. "It's just like movie editing—he'll cut or restructure scenes that have already been shot. If there's a moment that doesn't work, we'll find a different moment. We might move some plot point up earlier, or we'll change an intimate scene between two people by stealing shots from different parts of the scene. Through this editorial process we find how best to tell the story.

"For me personally, what I've learned from J.J., more than anything, is a love of moviemaking and a certain language of filmmaking. Right from the pilot there was a boldness that's inherent in a kind of filmmaking that's very American. It's hard to explain. Colors and characters come forward, they don't remain in the realm of the psychological. There's more of a heroic and visceral quality to the characters' behavior."

Contributing to the emotional impact of each episode was another key aspect of post-production—the musical score. And here again, *Alias* sought to bring a feature-film feel to the smaller-than-life world inside the TV screen.

# THE MUSIC MAN

In the converted garage of a home on a quiet residential street a short drive from the Disney studio, *Alias* music is masterminded. Composer Michael

*Alias* composer Michael Giacchino relaxes in the studio of his company, Edgewater Park Music. "When I first talked to J.J., I said I didn't want *Alias* to sound like a TV show, and he totally agreed with that," Giacchiano recalled. "We wanted the music to be big and different and to sound like a feature film."

**Space enthusiast Giacchino aboard NASA's space shuttle *Atlantis* during a visit to Edwards Air Force Base.**

Giacchino's studio is air-conditioned, cool, and cozy. On the wall by his keyboard and computer monitor are two side-by-side clocks, one to tick off the local hour, the other to show the time on the East Coast, where Giacchino's parents live. One of the clock's batteries ran out of juice and the clock stopped at 8:46. The other clock stopped several months later—at exactly 8:46. Giacchino has left them there, frozen in time, his own believe-it-or-not items from the Twilight Zone of life.

Below the clocks is a snapshot of Giacchino aboard the space shuttle *Atlantis*—a photo taken on the ground, he hastens to explain—when the computer systems were being upgraded in 1998. The visit to *Atlantis* was a special reward from DreamWorks Interactive for the hard work of Giacchino and fellow game creators. Giacchino had been scoring the music for such DreamWorks PlayStation games as the World War II–themed Medal of Honor, which also happened to be a favorite of *Alias* writer Jesse Alexander. Alexander didn't know Giacchino but loved the game's music and recommended its composer to J. J. Abrams. Thus, one night, Giacchino received an e-mail that began: "Hi, my name is J. J. Abrams. . . ."

A sample Giacchino score sheet, produced for the pilot episode's "Parking Garage" chase sequence.

**ALIAS - Parking Garage**

Composed by Michael Giacchino

**The *Alias* orchestra assembles at Paramount's Stage M.**

"I met with J.J. when they were getting ready to shoot the pilot and Jennifer Garner was doing costume tests," Giacchino recalled. "We'd be talking as Jennifer kept coming in dressed in different costumes—here's the one for the funeral, here's the one for the break-in—and J.J. would go, 'I like this. . . . I like that.' It was very surreal. But it worked out nicely. J.J. liked the music on the games because it was done with a live orchestra and felt like old movies, with a big sound and everybody having their own theme music. I then did the *Alias* pilot with a live orchestra, which is something I love."

In the early decades of television, music was always recorded with a live orchestra, but with the advent of electronic music it became almost reflex for productions to rely on synthesized samples of musical instruments. "Synth never sounds as good," Giacchino declared. "What's great about *Alias* is ninety-nine percent of the music is live. We actually go into the studio and record with a fifty-piece orchestra composed of studio players from the L.A. area."

POST–PRODUCTION: PUTTING IT TOGETHER

**133**

The *Alias* music included what Giacchino called a techno-element, from the jazzy electronic *Alias* theme created by J. J. Abrams himself to Sydney Bristow's signature sound, and even compositions blending techno beats with live instrumentals. The episodes' distant, exotic settings also allowed the composer to include musical echoes from all over the planet, from instruments unique to a particular culture to music indigenous to a particular place (such as a bit of Puccini flavoring the Vatican break-in episode). Sometimes the music paid homage to the show's spy motif, such as the "John Barry–style James Bond jazz riff" Giacchino used for Sydney Bristow's entrance into a Vegas casino.

Recording engineer Dan Wallin (right) recording at an *Alias* orchestral session at the Paramount Studios Stage M scoring stage.

The range of *Alias* music was considerable, as were the demands—an average of twenty-five minutes per episode, Giacchino estimated. Episodic television dictated an intense work schedule for the composer, as it did for everyone else. Giacchino's week began on Friday, as the edited episode was being finalized. Earlier that day, Abrams and Giacchino would meet in the editing suite at Disney to watch a rough cut and plan what kind of music might work where. "The use of music depends on the scene, it's a very subjective process," Giacchino explained. "Some scenes play best without music. If it's a scene pushing some action or a time lapse, music helps spell that out for the audience."

By Saturday morning a "locked" copy of the episode would be waiting on Giacchino's doorstep. "'Locked' means nobody can touch it," Giacchino explained. "The music needs to be lined up correctly and hit all the various points throughout the show, so when I lay in the music I need a version that's not going to change. I'd prepare all the sheet music through the weekend and we'd have Tuesday to record everything."

While his friend and colleague Tim Simonec conducted an orchestra that included brass, wind, and string sections, Giacchino sat behind the glass of the recording-studio control booth. Both conductor and composer would wear headphones, so that Giacchino could communicate feedback or instructions. Meanwhile, as recording engineer Dan Wallin worked on getting a good stereo mix, each instrument played into its own microphone, ultimately making for twenty-four tracks. Those separate recordings allowed for later manipulation of any one instrument, if necessary.

By Tuesday night, Giacchino was typically back in his studio working on the final mix, using one of his two Mackie twenty-four-track digital recorders. "The violin section, for example, will be split up into two tracks. Same with violas, cellos, bass, wind instruments," Giacchino explained. "But ninety percent of the time Dan gets such a great live sound at the recording session I don't have to change anything."

It's a mystery about music—why does it work so well with movie and television storytelling? "When you're breaking up with your girlfriend no

**Conductor Tim Simonec, Michael Giacchino, and son Mick take a break at the scoring stage.**

one is behind you singing," Giacchino laughed. "It's crazy. It would never be there in real life but, for some reason, music in movies or television has that drama and you accept it. It worked for opera, too. For some reason we're able to tell stories through music."

what it is, her voice is so gone.  Suit and Glasses didn't
hear.

                         SUIT AND GLASSES
              Louder.

                         SYDNEY
                    (crying)
                    ... I can't...

Suit and Glasses moves closer than ever -- grabbing her
face, which is the sharpest pain for Sydney --

                         SUIT AND GLASSES
              Who do you work for... you pretty
              little girl?

He moves closer when suddenly she VIOLENTLY HEAD-BUTTS him -
- with such force that Suit and Glasses falls back, semi-
conscious before he can hit the ground.  Sydney springs to
life, swooping the chair UNDER HER and down upon Suit and
Glasses -- the support bar of the chair shoved into his
neck --

# THE FIRST SEASON

## PILOT: "TRUTH BE TOLD"

AIRDATE: 9.30.01

WRITER AND DIRECTOR: J. J. ABRAMS

STORY: Sydney Bristow tells her fiancé, Danny Hecht, about her alias as an SD-6 secret agent—and he's murdered on order of SD-6 head Arvin Sloane. Sydney discovers she's not working for a covert arm of the CIA but a rogue agency and that her father is a double agent at SD-6, secretly spying for the CIA. Sydney similarly accepts a double-agent assignment to achieve her goal of bringing down SD-6.

HIGHLIGHTS: That red wig Sydney wears, and a mission to Taipei, where she's tortured by the menacing mystery man known in the script as Suit and Glasses.

COOL GADGETS: A cigarette lighter that can disrupt any video signal within a 420-yard radius . . . lipstick that's really a camera that takes pictures and measures space in three axes from one vantage point . . .

# EPISODE 2. "SO IT BEGINS"

AIRDATE: 10.07.01
WRITER: J. J. ABRAMS
DIRECTOR: KEN OLIN

**OPENER:** Sydney learns from her CIA handler, Agent Vaughn, that SD-6 is not just the subterranean Los Angeles office located under the downtown bank Credit Dauphine, but a tangled web encompassing over two hundred groups.

**MISSION:** In Moscow, Sydney steals computer files for SD-6 regarding Russia's Cold War–era nuclear arsenal. For her CIA countermission Sydney executes a "brush pass" of the nuke info with Vaughn at LAX, allowing the CIA to make a copy and return the original to her—all before she and Dixon leave LAX.

**COOL GADGETS:** A silver box disguised as a video scrambler . . . a ring with a hidden jewel that contains a sedative powerful enough to make a person pass out on contact . . .

**PERSONAL STORIES:** Jack Bristow reveals to Sydney that he tried to save Danny's life. Meanwhile, Will Tippin, Sydney's close friend and an L.A. newspaper reporter, begins investigating Danny's death.

**CLIFFHANGER:** Sydney digs up a missing nuclear bomb in a Virginia cemetery—and realizes she's activated it! Only frantic cell-phone instructions from Marshall, the high-tech wizard at SD-6, on how to deactivate the bomb avert disaster. SD-6 gets the nuke and Sydney tries to get it back for the CIA, a mission that leads her to Cairo and ruthless arms dealer Ineni Hassan—who has a gun pointed at Sydney's head at episode's end.

# EPISODE 3. "PARITY"

AIRDATE: 10.14.01
WRITERS: ALEX KURTZMAN AND ROBERTO ORCI
DIRECTOR: MIKAEL SALOMON

**OPENER:** Sydney distracts Hassan and makes her escape with the nuclear bomb's core.

**MISSION:** Sydney beats Anna Espinosa, her enemy at the rival K-Directorate spy agency, to a vault in Madrid, where she obtains a lockbox. Inside is a sketch by fifteenth-century scientist and seer Milo Rambaldi—the chase for the puzzle pieces of Rambaldi artifacts is on!

**WILL'S INVESTIGATION:** Will requests surveillance footage from traffic cameras around Danny's former apartment on the night of the murder and discovers that the cameras went out on that night.

**COOL GADGETS:** A pearl necklace with a microphone inside the pendant . . . a Spanish pesata coin that's actually a sonic wave emitter with a remote trigger—a pen Sydney has . . .

**PERSONAL STORIES:** Vaughn is removed as Sydney's handler but is reinstated at Sydney's demand. Will kisses Sydney and gets a let's-just-be-friends reaction. Meanwhile, Sydney's friend Francie is having her own boyfriend troubles.

**CLIFFHANGER:** Anna has the key to the lockbox, and SD-6 arranges for Sydney to meet up with her at a Berlin stadium so they can view the sketch together. When Anna opens the lockbox, both agents are horrified as a sizzling sound comes from inside. . . .

## EPISODE 4, "A BROKEN HEART"

AIRDATE: 10.21.01
WRITER: VANESSA TAYLOR
DIRECTOR: HARRY WINER

**OPENER/RAMBALDI MYSTERY:** In Berlin, Sydney and Anna each have seconds to memorize a five-hundred-year-old Rambaldi binary code before it self-destructs. The code leads them to a church in Málaga, Spain, where Sydney removes a round crystal from a stained-glass window. The crystal is later revealed to be a presynthetic polymer from the mind of Rambaldi.

**MISSION:** During a mission to track Luc Jacqnoud in Cairo, an SD-6 contact and friend of Sydney's is killed. Back home, Jack Bristow is getting the third degree from SD-6 interrogator Agent McCullough. Sydney and Dixon then jet to Sao Paolo and the United Commerce Organization conference, where Sydney witnesses Edgar Peace Prize winner Dhiren Patel getting a pacemaker bomb implanted by mastermind Jacqnoud.

**CLIFFHANGER:** A bodyguard who Sydney beat up in Cairo discovers her spying and knocks her unconcious.

**COOL GADGETS:** A parabolic microphone disguised as a travel pouch . . . a telescope disguised as a pen. . .

## EPISODE 5, "DOPPELGÄNGER"

AIRDATE: 10.28.01
WRITER: DANIEL ARKIN
DIRECTOR: KEN OLIN

**OPENER:** Sydney and Dixon take over an ambulance carrying Patel. Dixon surgically removes the bomb and throws it in the path of Jacqnoud's car, with explosive results.

**WILL'S INVESTIGATION:** Will meets Kate Jones, who claims to have had an affair with Danny. The problem is that according to her social security number, Kate Jones died in 1973.

**MISSION:** SD-6 wants info on a Hensel Corporation vaccine from company scientist Jeroen Schiller. Sydney pulls the ultimate switch, giving the CIA the real Schiller and SD-6 a CIA plant. Sloane suspects, but info from the real Schiller as to the location of vaccine inhalers in a German plant—and convincing arm twisting from Jack—preserves the impostor Schiller's cover.

**COOL GADGETS:** A business card that works as a transmitter . . . a crate that's outfitted to ship a human being . . . a microchip-controlled box that overrides alarm systems. . .

**BAD NEWS:** Sydney and Dixon retrieve the inhalers from the plant in Badenweiler, Germany. Sydney secretly defuses a bomb they've planted, but Dixon uses a secondary detonator to blow up the plant—with secret CIA agents still inside.

# EPISODE 6, "RECKONING"

AIRDATE: 11.18.01
WRITER: JESSE ALEXANDER
DIRECTOR: DANIEL ATTIAS

**PERSONAL STORIES:** Back at SD-6, Sydney is told her father will be working alongside her. Vaughn tells Sydney his father died serving the CIA. But looking into Jack's CIA file raises Sydney's suspicions about her father's loyalties.

**WILL'S INVESTIGATION:** Will learns that the name of the woman claiming to be Kate Jones is actually Eloise Kurtz. When he confronts her, he gets a blast of pepper spray. But when he arrives at her apartment he discovers she's skipped out.

**MISSION:** Sydney and Dixon's recovery of a genetically secured encoder device requires a DNA fingertip sample from one Gareth Parkashoff.

**PROBLEM:** Parkashoff has been murdered. Only his killer, an FTL agency assassin named Martin Shepard, knows where the body is buried, and Shepard is locked away in the Mangalev Asylum, a grim Bucharest, Romania, mental institution.

**BAD NEWS:** Marshall discovers a CIA worm in the SD-6 mainframe. Upon hearing of the breach, Sloane is convinced that's there's a mole in SD-6.

**COOL GADGETS:** Green thermal sunglasses that can see behind walls . . . a digital watch disguising a safe-cracking decoder . . .

**CLIFFHANGER:** Sydney goes undercover as a mental patient to get to Shepard but discovers the asylum is being run by K-Directorate agent Kreshnik—and finds the agent assigned to the mission with her murdered in Kreshnik's office.

# EPISODE 7, "COLOR-BLIND"

AIRDATE: 11.25.01
WRITERS: ROBERTO ORCI AND ALEX KURTZMAN
DIRECTOR: JACK BENDER

OPENER/REVELATION: Sydney breaks out of Mangalev with Shepard. In a CIA safehouse she helps Shepard break through his repressed memories, only to discover a shocking truth—Shepard had been programmed by SD-6 and was Danny's killer.

PERSONAL STORIES: Jack interrupts Sydney's Thanksgiving dinner to privately tell her he was investigated by the FBI as a KGB suspect twenty years before, when an FBI pursuit forced his car off the road and into a river. (Jack escaped, but Sydney's mother, Laura, was lost and presumed dead in the rushing river.) Jack shows Sydney a letter from the FBI, clearing him of any connection to the KGB. Charlie proposes to Francie, who accepts.

RAMBALDI MYSTERY: The Parkashoff DNA, decoded by SD-6, reveals a communiqué about a Rambaldi artifact, a clock under analysis at Oxford. Sydney must get it—before K-Directorate's Anna Espinosa.

SD-6 POLITICS: Sloane talks with Alain Christophe about the suspected moles at SD-6—could it be Jack and/or Sydney?

# EPISODE 8, "TIME WILL TELL"

AIRDATE: 12.02.01
WRITER: JEFF PINKNER
DIRECTOR: PERRY LANG

OPENER: Sydney grabs the Rambaldi clock while Jack confronts Sloane about the murder of Eloise Kurtz, the woman Jack hired to impersonate Kate Jones and whom Sloane ordered killed.

COOL GADGETS: A phone disguising a biometric sensor with a fingerprint-scanning digitizer . . . perfume with a temporary sedative . . .

RAMBALDI MYSTERY: Sloane sends Sydney to Positano, Italy, to have the

Rambaldi clock, built in 1503, repaired by a descendant of Rambaldi's clock maker, Giovanni Donato. The mysterious old man repairs the clock moments before he's killed by a K-Directorate sniper who was aiming at Sydney.

**SD-6 POLITICS:** A mole is suspected inside the agency, and a functional imaging test administered to Sydney by SD-6 Agent Karl Dreyer—and Sydney's too-perfect answers—leads him to conclude she is that mole.

**WILL'S INVESTIGATION:** Will finds a mysterious pin in the murdered Eloise Kurtz's car. A techy-friend tells him it's government/intelligence issue.

**PERSONAL STORIES:** Sydney discovers that the pages of a book her father gave her mother are secretly embedded with a Russian code, increasing her suspicions that Jack was KGB.

**COOL GADGETS:** A black purse that works like an X-ray machine . . .

**MISSION/CLIFFHANGER:** Marshall discovers that the presynthetic polymer from the church in Málaga fits into the repaired Rambaldi clock and reveals a star chart and specific location on Mount Aconcagua, near the border of Chile and Argentina. There Sydney and Dixon discover an underground chamber and a book marked with the Rambaldi symbol: <0>. But Anna appears, snatching the book and knocking Sydney off a ladder, seemingly to her death.

# EPISODE 9, "MEA CULPA"

AIRDATE: 12.09.01
WRITERS: DEBRA J. FISHER AND ERICA MESSER
DIRECTOR: KEN OLIN

**OPENER:** Sydney survives the fall, miraculously becoming entangled on a rung of the ladder. Back and unable to contact SD-6, on the ground, she uses a CIA satellite phone to get Dixon to a hospital. But she wonders— has Dixon overheard her call for CIA backup?

**MISSION:** Sydney goes to Tuscany to steal Ineni Hassan's offshore account numbers from his accountant. Hassan has betrayed SD-6 and Sloane wants to freeze the arms dealer's accounts.

**SD-6 POLITICS:** Sloane orders Sydney's assassination, a "kill order" on a worm channel that the CIA intercepts. Agent Vaughn has a team in place to rescue Sydney, but Jack tells him it's a trap to expose whether Sydney is really a double agent. The CIA stands down, Sydney emerges unscathed, and Sloane is convinced she's still a loyal SD-6 operative.

**WILL'S INVESTIGATION:** Will visits his tech friend who tells him the pin is an active listening device, and is still on. Will talks into the pin, trying to contact whoever is on the other end. Will is contacted, called on the phone by a mysterious person, and given a cassette-tape recording of Eloise Kurtz's execution-style murder.

**MISSION:** SD-6 discovers that the numbers stolen from Tuscany only contained part of Hassan's bank account info. Sydney and fellow SD-6 colleague Agent Ernesto Russek go to Geneva to get the account numbers. Mission accomplished, Sydney simultaneously beams the numbers to SD-6 and, secretly, to the CIA. Back home, Marshall discovers the secret transmission and reports it to Agent Dreyer.

**COOL GADGETS:** A phone disguising a biometric sensor with a fingerprint-scanning digitizer . . . perfume with a temporary sedative . . .

**CLIFFHANGER:** After visiting Dixon, who's recovering in the hospital, Sydney is captured on Sloane's orders. Dyer is still convinced Sydney is the mole.

# EPISODE 10, "SPIRIT"

AIRDATE: 12.16.01
WRITERS: J. J. ABRAMS AND VANESSA TAYLOR
DIRECTOR: JACK BENDER
NOTABLE GUEST STAR'S FIRST APPEARANCE:
KEN OLIN AS DAVID MCNEIL

**OPENER:** Sydney is taken to an SD-6 torture room, but the interrogation is halted. Instead, Russek is tortured in her place, and killed. Sloane tells a shocked Sydney there was an intercepted communication in Geneva revealing Russek sent the numbers to K-Directorate.

**PERSONAL STORIES:** Vaughn gives Sydney an antique frame as a Christmas gift. Will is jealous but can't complain—he's begun an office romance with his assistant, Jenny.

**MISSION:** Sydney goes to Semba Island off the coast of Kenya and discovers Hassan has had plastic surgery and is going under the name Nebseni Saad. Sloane knows this and also that Hassan is in Cuba, where he sends Jack with kill orders. But Jack's CIA counterorders are to get Hassan into protection so the arms dealer can supply the agency with his client list.

**WILL'S INVESTIGATION:** Nevil, an audio engineer, discovers some muffled dialogue on the tape Will found in his car and deciphers a mysterious word—SD-6. Will finds an SD-6 reference in the transcripts of a lawsuit against a David McNeil, a businessman who developed a computer encryption program who's in prison for embezzlement. McNeil's lawyer tells Will that McNeil's wife killed herself under mysterious circumstances. Will visits McNeil in jail and scares off the inmate at the mention of SD-6.

**COOL GADGETS:** "Super-swank" pink-lensed sunglasses with a silent telephoto camera . . . a cell phone that dispenses a keycard for opening most hotel door locks . . .

**CLIFFHANGER:** Sydney learns from Vaughn that her father doctored the transmissions to implicate Russek. Vaughn also reveals that Jack is being held captive by Hassan in Cuba. Sydney goes to rescue him and is her-

self captured. Hassan, who doesn't know Jack and Sydney are related, gives Jack a gun and orders him to prove he is who he says by killing Sydney.

## EPISODE 11, "THE CONFESSION"

AIRDATE: 1.6.02
WRITERS: J. J. ABRAMS AND DANIEL ARKIN
DIRECTOR: HARRY WINER

OPENER: In a synchronized attack, Jack and Sydney overpower Hassan and deliver him into CIA protection. They then fake photos to convince Sloane the arms dealer is dead.

PERSONAL STORIES: Vaughn tells Sydney that the codes embedded in the books Jack bought her mother were KGB orders with names of CIA agents who were killed years ago. They later discuss the codes and, as they become more convinced that Jack was KGB, Vaughn secretly tapes their conversation.

MISSION: Sydney and Dixon travel to Greece to swipe from Hassan associate Minos Sakkoulas computer files that will lead to a device called the Package. Sydney's countermission is to give the CIA the real information and give fake files to SD-6. Sydney fails, with Dixon downloading the info for SD-6.

PERSONAL STORIES: Vaughn reveals to Sydney he taped their earlier conversation—and that his father was one of those murdered agents mentioned in the secret code book. A distraught Sydney retreats to Will's comforting arms.

MISSION: Hassan reveals to Vaughn that the Package is hidden in an abandoned missile silo on Crete. Sydney goes there, but Hassan, angry at the CIA's refusal to bring his wife and son to the U.S. for protection, provides a false code to the alarm system. The alarm activates an anti-intruder device that soaks the bunker with gasoline with Sydney imprisoned inside. Vaughn and his assistant, Agent Weiss, scramble to get high-level approval to protect Hassan's family, and the arms dealer gives the correct code, which shuts down the anti-intruder mechanism. Sakkoulas discov-

ers Sydney in the bunker, but she escapes with the Package just as a spark ignites the gasoline, killing Sakkoulas.

COOL GADGETS: Red-tinted sunglasses with high-resolution retina scanners . . . a camera disguised as a compact . . . lipstick voice recorder . . .

REVELATION/CLIFFHANGER: At a high-level CIA meeting, which Sydney and Vaughn attend, Jack Bristow reveals that that he was never a KGB agent—Sydney's mother was! Jack is not the agent who carried out the hits on CIA agents . . . it was Laura Bristow.

# EPISODE 12, "THE BOX" (PART 1)

AIRDATE: 1.20.02
WRITERS: JESSE ALEXANDER AND JOHN EISENDRATH
DIRECTOR: JACK BENDER
NOTABLE GUEST STAR'S FIRST APPEARANCE:
QUENTIN TARANTINO AS MCKENAS COLE
PATRICIA WETTIG AS DR. JUDY BARNETT

OPENER: Sydney wants out of the spy game after learning the truth about her mother, but Jack warns that if Sloane doesn't have her killed, then Sloane's superiors within the umbrella organization, the Alliance, will.

WILL'S INVESTIGATION: Will decides the SD-6 story is too dangerous to pursue and ignores an envelope left for him at his office. But the mystery "Deep Throat" voice in the pin transmitter tells him not to give up.

McNeil's daughter Kelly finally persuades him to continue his investigation. Will opens the envelope—and discovers a key inside.

**PERSONAL STORIES:** Vaughn is questioned by CIA psychiatrist Dr. Barnett as to the propriety of his giving a Christmas gift to Agent Sydney Bristow. Vaughn confronts the man who informed Barnett about the gift, fellow agent Haladki.

**THE COUP:** Jack and Sydney are trapped in an SD-6 elevator and realize emergency lockdown procedures have been enacted, which can mean only one thing—SD-6 is under siege! A group of intruders have swiftly put the entire staff under armed guard, while their leader, an ex-SD-6 agent named McKenas Cole, prepares to torture Sloane for the access codes to the SD-6 vaults. But, unknown to Cole, if the vault is opened while in lockdown, security measures will detonate an explosion that'll bring down the entire building.

**COOL GADGETS:** Cole's gadgets: Needles of Fire—needles covered with a toxic substance used on Sloane . . . Heartbeat monitors which locate people by reading their heartbeats . . .

**SYDNEY'S GADGETS:** An earring that's a tiny grenade . . .

**CLIFFHANGER:** Jack tells Sydney that a scrambling device in Marshall's workshop will prevent the vault from being opened. Sydney gets it and applies the scrambler to the vault door just as Cole and his armed cohorts arrive. They hear her in the airshaft and blast away.

# EPISODE 13, "THE BOX" (PART 2)

AIRDATE: 2.10.02
WRITERS: JESSE ALEXANDER AND JOHN EISENDRATH
DIRECTOR: JACK BENDER
**OPENER:** Jack surrenders, allowing Sydney to remain hidden. The intruders try to hack the vault security code, so Sydney must disarm the three C-4 charges that comprise the fail-safe system. Meanwhile, in a daring move, Agent Dixon has secretly signaled the CIA's L.A. bureau office as

to SD-6's predicament. Vaughn wants to move in, but Agent Haladki, now in charge of the SD-6 case, refuses.

MISSION: Sydney and Jack work to save SD-6 from destruction. Agent Vaughn disobeys orders and goes to SD-6. He meets up with Sydney and together they disarm two of the C-4 charges. But Sydney is forced to surrender before they can disarm the last charge. In a synchronized move, Sydney, Dixon, Marshall, and Jack overpower their guards—but Cole remains at large.

WILL'S INVESTIGATION: Will uses the key in the envelope to open a locker containing the autopsy report on David McNeil's wife, which reveals that her death was not a suicide. Will urges Kelly McNeil to go into hiding.

MISSION: Agent Weiss learns that Vaughn has called Haladki and that the SD-6 office has been attacked. Vaughn's not sure whether Haladki will help. In response, Weiss insists that the CIA send a rescue team. Meanwhile, Jack discovers a bound Sloane in the torture room, where Cole has been trying to extract the vault's code through the pain pricks of his needles of fire. With time ticking away before the vault opens and ignites the final C-4 explosive charge, the only way to stop the explosion is cancelling it at Sloane's desk—but only Sloane's fingerprint can activate the cancel order. Sloane orders Jack to cut off his finger and to use the fingerprint to verify cancellation of the fail-safe order at Sloane's desk. Jack does so, moments before Cole opens the vault and removes a metal box marked with the Rambaldi symbol. But the CIA rescue team captures the escaping Cole and takes possession of the Rambaldi artifact— a small vial of liquid. Sloane waits for medics to have his finger reattached.

COOL GADGETS: An electromagnetic clamp that can break a secured door's magnetic seal . . . a razor-prism that can cut into fiber-optic cable without disrupting the data stream . . . a bugged ring . . .

## EPISODE 14, "THE COUP"

AIRDATE: 2.24.02
WRITERS: ALEX KURTZMAN AND ROBERTO ORCI
DIRECTOR: TOM WRIGHT

OPENER: On the day of the assault on SD-6, the heads of rival agency FTL were attacked and wiped out in Hong Kong by an unknown group that has contacted K-Directorate to share information regarding another stolen Rambaldi artifact. The artifact is a matter of supreme importance to Sloane. He thanks Sydney for saving SD-6 and tries to comfort her about her mother being a KGB agent.

MISSION: Sydney and Dixon must find out the time and location of the meeting between the mystery group and K-Directorate. To do so, Sydney and Dixon go to Las Vegas to plant a listening device on a K-Directorate agent. Dixon, posing as a Jamaican diplomat, enters into a high-stakes card game with the agent while Sydney, who has gained entry disguised as a cocktail waitress, hacks into the casino surveillance system to monitor the cards and transmit the pertinent information to Dixon through his hidden listening device. Dixon goads the agent to wager his ring, which he switches for a duplicate bugged ring.

PERSONAL STORIES: Sydney's cover is almost blown as she discovers that Francie and her boyfriend, Charlie, have come to Vegas, where they hope to run into Sydney, who'd told them she'd be there on bank business. While watching the surveillance monitor during the card game, Sydney discovers that Charlie and Francie are about to get married in a casino chapel. Sydney has already learned that Charlie has been cheating on Francie, so she leaves her post (after asking Dixon to stall) to privately confront Charlie about his philandering, leading to the cancellation of the quickie wedding. Later Sydney tells Francie about Charlie's infidelity.

WILL'S INVESTIGATION: McNeil tells Will that software he designed includes a "back-door program," a virtual guest book of anyone who's used his software. Will sneaks into McNeil's old company to download it, providing him with another clue in the deepening mystery of SD-6.

CLIFFHANGER: The planted bug reveals that the unknown group and K-Directorate will meet in Moscow. Sydney and Dixon go there, where a Mr. Sark confronts Ilyich Ivankov, the head of K-Directorate, with an offer to buy the Rambaldi artifact. Ivankov scoffs at the offer, but as he prepares to leave, he is killed, and Sark finishes the negotiation with Lavro Kessar, a remaining K-Directorate lieutenant. Sydney has seen it all, peering through a window while dangling from a tension wire attached to a nearby building. But a guard below, alerted to her presence, opens fire.

COOL GADGETS: A parasail . . . a digital camera . . .

# EPISODE 15, "PAGE 47"

AIRDATE: 3.3.02
WRITER: J. J. ABRAMS AND JEFF PINKNER
DIRECTOR: KEN OLIN
NOTABLE GUEST STAR'S FIRST APPEARANCE:
AMY IRVING AS EMILY SLOANE
OPENER: As bullets zing past her, Sydney swings on her wire back through the window of the adjacent building and makes her escape with Dixon,

along with video of the fateful meeting. Meanwhile, Sloane tells Jack that the noisy reporter Will Tippin must be "silenced."

**PERSONAL STORIES:** Francie tells Sydney she's confronted Charlie about his womanizing and broken off their engagement. Sydney reveals she still wears the engagement ring Danny gave her. In a personal ritual, the two friends remove their rings.

**MISSION:** Sydney and Dixon travel to Tunisia, where they intercept the Rambaldi manuscript—swiped by Anna during the mission to Mount Aconcagua—just before it's to be transferred to Mr. Sark. In her countermission, Sydney photographs the ancient manuscript for the CIA. Meanwhile, Vaughn gets Sydney to use her friendship with Sloane's wife, Emily, who's sick with cancer, to elicit a dinner invitation to Sloane's house in order to plant a bug.

**COOL GADGETS:** A perfume bottle with tranquilizer spray . . . a safe-cracker disguised as lipstick . . .

**WILL'S INVESTIGATION:** Will is kidnapped by two masked men, who threaten to kill his family and friends if he continues his SD-6 investigation. One of those masked men is Jack, who has essentially saved Will's life. Will tells McNeil he can't risk the lives of those close to him, so he's abandoning the investigation. In an ironic twist, the unsuspecting Will meets his would-be executioner, Arvin Sloane, as Sydney's dinner date at the party at Sloane's house.

**REVELATION/CLIFFHANGER:** Before the dinner, Sydney has been told page 47 is missing from the recovered Rambaldi manuscript. At Sloane's house, Sydney opens a safe and retrieves the missing page moments before Sloane appears. Later, Vaughn meets Sydney to tell her the liquid vial recovered from the SD-6 vault during the Cole break-in was a wash that has revealed an invisible image on page 47—a portrait of Sydney herself.

# EPISODE 16, "THE PROPHECY"

AIRDATE: 3.10.02
WRITER: JOHN EISENDRATH
DIRECTOR: DAVIS GUGGENHEIM
NOTABLE GUEST STAR'S FIRST APPEARANCE:
ROGER MOORE AS EDWARD POOLE

**OPENER:** The partially decoded Rambaldi manuscript page 47 details a prophecy of such consequence that the Department of Special Research, the paranormal research division of the National Security Agency, begins investigating Sydney's seeming connection to the ancient book and subjects her to a battery of tests.

**THE MAN:** Meanwhile, SD-6 has identified The Man—the shadowy superior of Cole and Mr. Sark—as Alexander Khasinau, ally of the Russian mob.

**THE ALLIANCE:** The twelve-member Alliance, the umbrella organization for SD-6 and eleven sister cells, must decide whether to have Khasinau killed or make peace. Sloane, furious at the SD-6 break-in Khasinau engineered, wants war. Edward Poole, head of SD-9, reveals to Sloane that John Briault, an Alliance member and potential swing vote, may be cooperating with Khasinau and should be eliminated.

RAMBALDI MYSTERY: The DSR continues its tests of Sydney Bristow. Sydney has agreed to cooperate because she wants to know the truth of her possible connection to the Rambaldi Prophecy. Jack reveals that the DSR doesn't have the original code key to Rambaldi's mystic musings. It's located in the Vatican and should be retrieved to reveal the true code. In a daring move, Sydney and Agent Vaughn break into the Vatican archives, and Sydney photographs the cryptic writing on a Rambaldi painting. Meanwhile, Sloane discovers that his page 47 of the Rambaldi manuscript is fake—does he suspect Sydney swiped the original?

THE ALLIANCE MEETS: Sloane personally and coldly murders his old friend Briault. But at the Alliance meeting, the resolution for war against Khasinau fails by one vote. Sloane realizes Poole, not Briault, is the one working with The Man. Sloane has killed his colleague for no reason.

THE PROPHECY: Sydney is taken into FBI custody. Vaughn is in the FBI van—he tells Sydney the CIA had the correct codekey in the first place and then he reads her the terrifying Prophecy: A woman with Sydney's characteristics will appear to "render the greatest power unto utter desolation."

COOL GADGETS: A parasail . . . a digital camera . . .

# EPISODE 17, "Q & A"

AIRDATE: 3.17.02
WRITER: J. J. ABRAMS
DIRECTOR: KEN OLIN

OPENER: FBI special officer Kendall and a team of interrogators question Sydney about her double-agent life. Jack tells Vaughn that if the interrogation goes on too long, her SD-6 cover will be blown.

MISSION: According to the Rambaldi writings, the woman in the Prophecy will never see Italy's Mount Subasio. If the CIA springs Sydney from her captors and she visits that mountain, claims that Sydney is the embodiment of the Prophecy will be nullified. Vaughn learns that Haladki is a former FBI agent and is maintaining contacts in the bureau and Jack, with brute force, convinces Haladki to reveal where the FBI is keeping Sydney.

REVELATION/CLIFFHANGER: Sydney is freed by Jack and Vaughn. As Sydney drives alone, in disguise, to the airport, tipped-off police squad cars converge and trap her at a dock—where she drives into the ocean. She survives at the bottom by sucking air from a tire valve. Later that night she meets her father to tell him that if she could survive that way, her mother might have done the same twenty years ago: Sydney's sure Rambaldi's Prophecy is about her mother . . . and that her mother is still alive.

# EPISODE 18, "MASQUERADE"

AIRDATE: 4.7.02
WRITER: ROBERTO ORCI AND ALEX KURTZMAN
DIRECTOR: CRAIG ZISK
NOTABLE GUEST STAR'S FIRST APPEARANCE:
PETER BERG AS NOAH HICKS

OPENER: Sydney travels to Italy and climbs Mount Subasio, thus disproving the theories that she is the incarnation of Rambaldi's Prophecy. Back home, her father confirms that the CIA are now searching for Laura Bristow in connection with the Prophecy. Jack has also learned that twenty years ago a CIA commission had concluded that Laura Bristow hadn't died, a fact that Sloane, then a CIA operative, has known all along.

MISSION: Sydney asks Sloane for a leave of absence to search for her mother. Sloane instead gives her a mission to Vienna to retrieve a microchip with data on Khasinau, explaining that by getting The Man, Sydney will find her mother—Khasinau was Laura's KGB superior. In Vienna, at a masked ball, Sydney retrieves the microchip with the help of Noah Hicks, an SD-6 agent and a former love before Danny.

**COOL GADGETS:** Diamond earrings that emit an infrared pulse . . . a camera that emits a high-intensity strobe light . . .

**PERSONAL STORIES:** Francie borrows one of Sydney's jackets and discovers an airplane ticket stub for Italy, not Seattle, where Sydney had said she went on a business trip. Meanwhile, Sydney confronts her father, who is shaken to his soul over the revelations about Laura. Sydney forces Jack into a trauma evaluation at the CIA.

**CLIFFHANGER:** Analysis of the microchip from Vienna sends Sydney and Noah on a mission to the Arkhangelsk Forest in Russia, where they must enter an underground complex to steal a computer data core detailing Khasinau's organization. Donning protective gear, Sydney enters a sub-zero cryo-chamber to get the data core and is almost killed as a robotics arm cracks her helmet and the cold nearly overcomes her. Noah rescues her and they escape to an SD-6 safehouse, where the former lovers—who earlier learned that their parting was a sad misunderstanding—ignite their smoldering passion.

# EPISODE 19, "SNOWMAN"

AIRDATE: 4.14.02
WRITER: JESSE ALEXANDER AND JEFF PINKNER
DIRECTOR: BARNET KELLMAN

**OPENER:** Sydney and Noah make a daring escape from Khasinau's soldiers. Back home, Vaughn informs Sydney that K-Directorate has hired "the Snowman," a mysterious assassin who favors an ice pick as a weapon, to take out Khasinau. Meanwhile, Noah reveals he has a secret bank account and wants Sydney to join him and leave the spy game.

**MISSION:** The data core is discovered to be worthless, although it contains grainy video files of Laura Bristow's debriefing, wherein the KGB femme fatale—real name Irina Derevko—reveals she was recruited to the KGB in 1970 by Khasinau and that marrying Jack was a strategic move. In the video are Khasinau and a man Sydney discovers to be Igor Valenko. Valenko worked undercover as FBI agent Bently Calder and allegedly pursued Laura Bristow during her car crash. Sydney believes Valenko, who now does business with a bank in Cape Town, South Africa, might still be a link to The Man. Through Jack's intervention and with Sloane's approval, Sydney and Noah head to a South African warehouse and hack into a computer, only to discover that the hard drive's memory has been lost.

COOL GADGETS: Armbands with boxes that perform active noise control . . . lipstick with a homing beacon and a waterproof cache . . .

PERSONAL STORIES: Francie and Will confront Sydney about the plane ticket to Italy. Sydney convinces her two concerned friends that she has simply been doing sensitive assignments for special bank clients—she's not in trouble and is doing nothing illegal. Her friends seem reassured, but Sydney has another lie on her conscience. Later, Noah, on a secret assignment, again asks Sydney to run away with him. Jack watches the Irina video and is devasted when she reveals she spied on him for ten years and considered him a complete fool.

REVELATION: SD-6 tech master Marshall has gleaned some low-level data from the South African hard drive, which leads Sydney and Dixon to Valenko's mansion in Mackay, Australia. Vaughn, who has been on the trail of the Snowman as a lead to Khasinau, learns that the feared assassin has been spotted in Mackay but has no way to contact Sydney. At Valenko's mansion, Sydney discovers the masked Snowman, who has killed his way through the house. In hand-to-hand combat, the assassin falls on a kitchen knife, and as he dies, Sydney pulls off his mask—revealing Noah Hicks.

# EPISODE 20, "THE SOLUTION"

AIRDATE: 4.21.02
WRITER: JOHN EISENDRATH
DIRECTOR: DAN ATTIAS

OPENER: Sydney, devasted by Hicks's death, confesses to Vaughn she doesn't know who to trust anymore, that in her quest to defeat SD-6, "I am becoming what I despised."

WILL'S INVESTIGATION: Will's "Deep Throat" calls and tell him he has enough on SD-6 to publish, then adds a kicker: One of the masked men who kidnapped and threatened him was Jack Bristow. Will confronts Jack in a bar about his Deep Throat contact and knowledge of SD-6. Jack suspects that Will's source is Agent Haladki and reports his suspicions to Devlin—but is admonished for being too "off book" of late. Jack secretly meets with Will and agrees to a partnership to get Deep Throat. Will is relieved when Jack tells him that Sydney has nothing to do with espionage.

SD-6 POLITICS/REVELATION: Emily Sloane's cancer has taken a turn for the worse, and she is hospitalized. Sydney visits Emily and is astonished when Sloane's wife reveals she's always known her husband works at SD-6. Unknown to them, the Alliance has bugged the hospital room. The commandment of complete secrecy about SD-6 has been broken and the mantra—knowledge [about SD-6] is like a virus, a virus must be contained—is presented to Sloane by an Alliance representative, suggesting that Sloane can prove he's in step with the Alliance by killing Emily himself.

MISSION: Sydney proposes to Vaughn that since Khasinau had made a failed attempt to get the vial of Rambaldi fluid from the SD-6 vaults, its obvious impostance to him could be used as a bait to smoke The Man out of hiding. Since Khasinau assumed Cole failed in his mission to get the vial from the vault, Sydney and Vaughn pull a heist of Rambaldi artifacts from a museum in Algeria. The high-profile crime leads Khasinau to assume the precious ampoule is now a potential black-market buy.

**COOL GADGETS:** A cell phone packed with plastic explosives . . .

**CLIFFHANGER:** Sydney and Vaughn travel to Denpassar, Indonesia, to make the Rambaldi sale with Mr. Sark, Khasinau's representative. Sydney is disguised in a native dress that covers her entire body except for her eyes. After proving her identity to Sark by pinning him in a duel with latajangs, Sydney's about to make the sale—and exchange a fake ampoule for the real one after Sark tests it—when Agent Dixon bursts in, holding them at gunpoint. As he looks at the woman and sees her eyes, he thinks he recognizes her. . . .

# EPISODE 21, "RENDEZVOUS"

AIRDATE: 5.5.02
WRITERS: DEBRA J. FISHER AND ERICA MESSER
DIRECTOR: KEN OLIN

**OPENER:** Vaughn creates a distraction and Sydney escapes, with Dixon in pursuit, while Vaughn retrieves the real vial from Sark.

**WILL'S INVESTIGATION:** Jack's plan for luring Deep Throat into the open is to have Will mention "The Circumference." Will does so and the mysterious voice agrees to a meeting, time and place to be determined.

**SD-6 POLITICS:** Sloane pleads with the Alliance to spare his wife's life. The Alliance, which has confirmed Edward Poole's connection to Khasinau, promises to consider Sloane's request—if he'll help find the elusive Khasinau. Sloane eventually meets with a captured Mr. Sark and seemingly convinces him to help SD-6 find The Man. The successful mission against Khasinau results in the Alliance letting Emily die of cancer instead of at an assassin's hands. But later, when Emily's cancer is suddenly found to be in remission, Sloane worries the Alliance may yet exact the supreme penalty. Meanwhile, Sydney, who was supposedly on a vacation trip into the desert during the incident in Denpassar, can't shake Dixon's suspicions. Her partner is starting to remember odd things . . . like the strange code and backup Sydney called for when he was down at Mount Aconcagua.

**MISSION:** Sloane informs Sydney and Dixon that they're to go to a Paris nightclub where Sark will be meeting with Khasinau, who has an office at the club. While The Man is occupied, they're ordered to not pick up Khasinau but steal a Rambaldi page from Khasinau's office safe. Meanwhile, Will gets the meeting place from Deep Throat. Will gets picked up at the meet spot and brought to the Paris nightclub where Sydney and Dixon have to swipe the Rambaldi artifact! An alarmed Sydney sees Will enter with Khasinau's men while Dixon is getting the Rambaldi page, she rescues her friend and takes him to a CIA safehouse.

**COOL GADGETS:** A ring that detects heartbeat signatures . . . non-lethal radioactive isotopes put in Sark's wine—they can be read by a geosynchronous satellite . . .

**CLIFFHANGER:** Sydney leaves Will at the safehouse. Suddenly, Sark breaks in, takes down the CIA men on watch, and shoots Will.

THE LAST EPISODE

# EPISODE 22, "ALMOST THIRTY YEARS"

AIRDATE: 5.12.02
WRITER: J. J. ABRAMS
DIRECTOR: J. J. ABRAMS

## ON-SET REPORT...

## SAN PEDRO, CALIFORNIA, 4.17.02...

## THE RETURN OF SUIT AND GLASSES

REVELATION: Sydney Bristow finally meets The Man—but it's not Khasinau. It's a room from a nightmare, a dirty, dark chamber in a welding shop crammed with grimy industrial junk. But it's also a place of exotica: Below an empty birdcage, a golden Buddha figurine sits atop a dusty counter where sweet smoke curls up to heaven from a tray of incense sticks. In the world of *Alias*, this is Taipei, and the workplace of the mysterious interrogator known only as Suit and Glasses.

Outside this chamber are the docks of San Pedro, a corner of the industrial zone of giant cranes and cargo ships that make up the Port of Los Angeles. The sun is going down, and some of the *Alias* crew are gathered by the outdoor craft service table. Bradley Cooper walks by, dressed in dirty jeans and a sweatshirt, eating a plate of meat loaf. He looks up and grins—one eye is swollen and bruised, and streaks of blood cake his face. It's Bradley in the makeup of Will Tippin, taking a break from hell.

To get back to hell one walks through an open warehouse door and a thick black curtain. Right there, in a cramped corner, is "Video Village," the station of black-and-white monitors that receives the feeds from the two cameras shooting this last episode of *Alias*'s first season. Chairs are drawn up around the monitors for director/writer J. J. Abrams, DP Michael Bonvillain, producer Sarah Caplan, script supervisor Tricia Goken, and other production principals. A few steps away is a short, dusty hallway leading to two closed doors and the torture chamber where Will is imprisoned. Standing in the aisle, looking immaculate in a dark suit and perfectly round spectacles, is Suit and Glasses himself. He looks up, his face a mask—and suddenly, the torturer's face melts away and actor Ric Young grins.

There's a little time to kill as Abrams, Bonvillain, cameramen Ross Judd and Chris Hayes, and the lighting crew prepare the torture chamber for a little bit of . . . dentistry without anesthesia. At the opposite end of the hallway is another thick black curtain. Young steps through it into a vast machine shop area that's unlit and practically deserted. Windows line the far walls, but night is falling fast and this airy space is falling with it, going deeper into darkness.

This final episode is for many of the crew and characters a coming full circle. It is so for Abrams, who has again scripted and is directing, book-ending the season with his writing and directorial work on the pilot. The pilot, of course, also marked the first appearance of Suit and Glasses, but then it was Sydney in the torture chair getting her tooth yanked, not poor Will. "I was so pleased that he's come back for the last episode—and he's still a mystery," Young says in a soft voice, settling back in a chair by the black curtain and musing about his character. "I think he'll always be a mystery.

In **"Almost Thirty Years,"** the first season's final episode, Will Tippin's reportorial instincts can't resist the lure of the shadowy world of espionage—and he suffers for it in the torture chamber of Suit and Glasses. **"Will is almost held captive by his ideals,"** Cooper muses about his character's willingness to put himself at risk. **"He's this ideal journalist, very idealistic—the truth has to matter."**

"He was such a strange character. When I first got the pilot script, the weird part was he didn't even have a name. It was just Suit and Glasses. Nobody knew anything about him. When a script gives you certain clues, like no name and you don't know anything about him, you begin to formulate a certain kind of a character. I suspected that since there are so many aliases in this show, and every character has a mystery about them, that this was another alias.

"So I really meditated a lot about this part. I imagined this monklike figure sitting absolutely still and just building up his energy until the moment comes that he's called for his missions and he comes into the outer world and then goes back into his own world. He comes from that dark place of timelessness and he moves in a very ethereal way, nothing is quite real and yet it is real. So, when I first got that, there was a lot of turning inwards to find that very dark place—and really enlighten it. There's a Zen sort of energy about this man who's very convinced about what he's doing and spiritual about it—he uses his inner power."

Young recalled how the pilot had him at ground zero for the launching of Garner's career (experienced though she was), into the rarefied heights of superstardom. "It was her first big role and she was amazing." Young smiled. "The moment I started working with her I knew she was going to make it because she can play action, comedy, tragedy. She has to show so much depth in her character because there are so many secrets and so much grief, and [as an actor] you've got to be clear on what you're holding back. The pain she shows in that incredible scene in the bathroom where she finds her murdered boyfriend is horrendous!

"It was wonderful working with Jennifer, but I was so scared that I'd really scare her, you know? There were moments I wanted to stop, because she was so convincing, the pain and horror of what I was doing to her—her face looking at me. As my character I couldn't betray that, but inside I was like, 'Oh, God—are you okay?' "

Young is sitting in shadow when the call comes that they're ready for the next scene. The torture-room set is crowded; the space around the torture chair that is the camera's focus is ringed with waiting actors (including Cooper, Young, and Sam Valdivia and Marcus Young as two uniformed Taiwanese guards), Bonvillain, cameramen Hayes and Judd, lighting crew and grips, property assistant Chris Redmond, first assistant director Noga Isackson, and others. J. J. Abrams is sitting by the Panavision cameras as the doors close and the call goes out for quiet. It's time to roll. . . .

"Energy— Action!" Abrams calls. The two guards walk into camera view, holding up a weary Will, who's slumped between them. They drop him into the chair and shackle him. Will pleads that "there's been . . . a major mistake." It's hard to watch his helplessness, his dawning horror, and some of those around the room avert their eyes.

"Be more scattered . . . ," Abrams calls out, the cameras still rolling, and Bradley plays his lines a different way. The chair scenes meld one into another, pieces of a larger fabric that includes Mr. Sark—actor David Anders—standing above Will and coldly intoning: "I have been instructed by my employer to keep you alive. But not comfortable. So I will ask you once. What is The Circumference?"

And then the two guards step in and yank Will's head up, and Ric Young, who's been standing out of camera range, settles his expression into the cold mask of Suit and Glasses and steps into the pool of light. He leans forward and whispers, "Hello." Bonvillain and Abrams direct the guards to move a certain way, for Young to lean slightly to one side to better catch the light. The scene plays out as clamps are fixed on Bradley's open mouth and Suit and Glasses extracts one of Will's teeth—and Cooper screams in gut-wrenching, bloodcurdling agony.

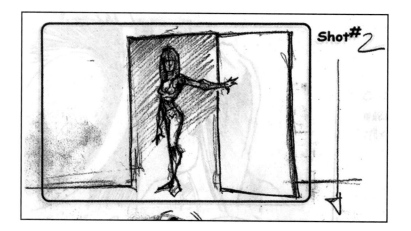

**Storyboards plotted out the dramatic, effects-filled sequence as Sydney and Vaughn discover the mysterious, massive Muller device, blow up its generator, and try to escape as a gigantic red antigravity ball liquefies and floods the device room. Visual effects supervisor Kevin Blank also had the rig for the miniatures-shoot side of the Muller device sequence.**

Shot # 7

Shot # 8

Mini
C.G.
g.s.

Shot # 9

Shot # 10

BALL

GUARDS

BACK
C.G.
g.s.

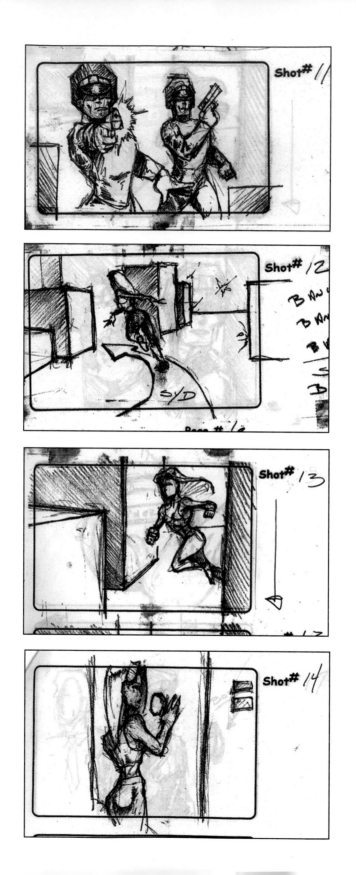

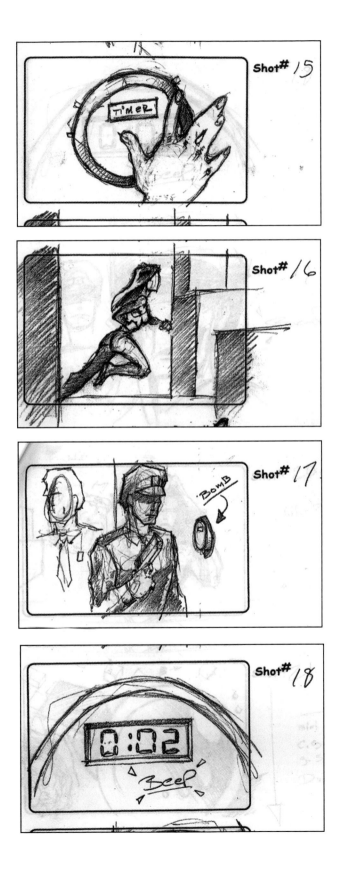

Shot # 15

Shot # 16

Shot # 17

"Bomb"

Shot # 18

0:02

Beep

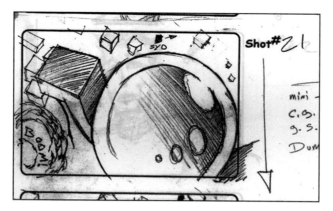

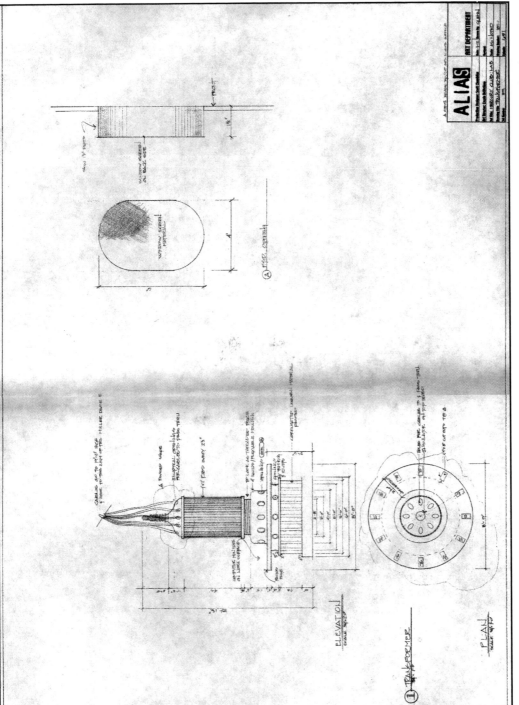

The art department's rough sketch and final production schematic of the "transformer," the power generator for the Muller device.

"You . . . had a cavity," Suit and Glasses says, turning to his tray of implements.

"Sick bastards," one of the crew murmurs, shaking his head and smiling as the shot cuts. Periodically, Cooper himself breaks the tension after a take, looking up and grinning through his blood-streaked mask.

Back at Video Village, Suit and Glasses looks spectral on the monitor screens, like some transmission from that timeless place the actor imagined. "It's so private," sighs Abrams, who's back at the monitor, reflecting on having once been alone with his words and now seeing them brought to life in all their gory glory.

Moving in and out of the room is makeup artist Diana Brown, a petite figure with her plastic makeup bag on her arm. She steps in between takes to freshen Cooper's blood. The post–tooth removal shots include a view of a battered Will dribbling blood. "I dreamed up the idea." Brown smiles sweetly, listing some of the elements of the makeup's design: a foam latex piece for the swollen eye, with a little glistening jelly added; "mouth blood" and dental cotton for swelling; molded plastic cuts. "The makeup helps the actors merge into their character. It adds something they can play with."

**Dueling camera face-off! J. J. Abrams gets caught during the final episode's late-night soundstage shoot at Disney. Note the transformer stage prop in the background.**

**Abrams near "Video Village" with script supervisor Tricia Goken. Behind them are the posted storyboards for the night's work, with each completed shot crossed out in red.**

Before the dinner break, Cooper—now a bloody mess, the red stains streaked along his sweatshirt like a Pollock painting—stands against a wall as Brown shoots Polaroids for continuity reference.

Dinner is served buffet style under the arching ceiling of an adjacent warehouse. Among the group are property assistants Chris Redmond and Sarah Bullion, and their conversation drifts into stories of the injury and even death that can happen when TV and movie crews work insane hours, day after day. "You're not frosty if you're working long hours. Mistakes happen," Redmond says.

This segment of the *Alias* shoot is demanding, with the workday stretching into the dawn hours, but the call times for the day's work to start are staggered to begin at early evening. Redmond explains the benefit of clear heads and clear thinking will be evident in the next shots, in which Will springs upon Suit and Glasses and jabs his tormentor with a syringe. Even though a retractable syringe will be used, the shot will be broken into two parts: the initial tackle, using the syringe without the needle—avoiding actually stabbing the performer—and a close-up for the retractable effect.

"Working on films is the next best thing to running away and joining the circus," Redmond concludes as the call comes to return to the set.

Abrams is back at Video Village while Ross Judd, a lean and wiry figure, straps himself into the vest and Steadicam arm of the "floating" camera with which he'll navigate the torture room. "'Pan-a-Mule,'" a passing Michael Bonvillain teases as Judd hoists up the heavy camera on the device's spring-loaded arm. Bonvillain raises what he claims is his thirtieth cup of green tea of the day and nods to Judd as the Steadicam operator begins

The transformer set on the Disney stage. Pictured in foreground: Juana Franklin, second assistant director (back to camera), and Noga Isackson, first assistant director. In the background, stunt coordinator Jeff Habberstad confers with a stunt person.

lining up the shot. "It's like, if you can't play the violin, a Stradivarius isn't going to do you any good. Ross is one of the best with the Steadicam, he moves like a dancer with that camera on his arm."

In the script, Suit and Glasses taunts Will that the truth serum he's about to inject him with can lead to "an unfortunate reaction" in one in five cases—little things like paralysis. Will then fakes paralysis in order to attack his tormentors, jabbing Suit and Glasses with the syringe and shouting "One in five!" as the guards pull him, kicking and fighting, out of the room. To get that action, fight coordinator David M. Morizot shows Cooper how he'll transition from pinning Suit and Glasses to throwing an elbow strike at the guards.

Sometime earlier, Cooper reflected on what he was bringing to the final episode, "the payoff of the whole year," as he called it. "The great thing about television is you're putting the bricks together, laying out this land-scape. At the beginning, you have to create the character. Now, every-thing I have to do physically as an actor has been done, and 'work' even becomes a hindrance. You just have to learn your lines, be relaxed and open, and it comes through because now you are that character. You have that history you've built up over twenty-one episodes."

The monitors at Video Village show the Steadicam moving in on a slumped-over Will, then circling as Suit and Glasses enters with the guards. The guards unshackle their victim—who leaps to the attack. "One in five!" Cooper cries, kicking and fighting—and the production principals encircling the monitors burst out laughing. Abrams leaps from his chair while calling out, "Print that!" as script supervisor Tricia Goken marks the instruction on "the Bible," her copy of the script upon which she's meticulously noted everything that's been shot or changed, forming a road map for the editors who will go through the night's footage.

But why is everybody laughing? Goken is still giggling as she explains it's just the sheer incongruous sight of Will Tippin becoming Mr. Action Hero and fighting back in the torture room.

The takes go on and on, with Abrams jumping back and forth shouting instructions, returning from the set to watch the action play out on the monitors. A crew member grins. "That set must be a shambles by now." It's surreal, the scene playing out on the black-and-white monitor as Will and the guards come out of frame—and crash, in real life, through the door into the narrow hallway adjacent to Video Village. After a half dozen takes, Cooper is looking exhausted. It's a massive expenditure of mental and physical energy being in that room, enduring torture and now having to physically wrestle with his tormentors.

The hour is getting late, and the cool night air outside is welcome after the confines of the torture chamber. The waterfront view is a vision seen in countless movies, that deathly still landscape of steel and concrete, mighty cranes and machinery—the kind of place where a torturer can go about his grim business in peace, without the prying eyes of conscience. There's a chill in the night air, and cawing seagulls are circling. . . .

### . . . ON-SET REPORT
### SAN PEDRO, CALIFORNIA, 04.18.02 . . .

### MIDNIGHT AT THE MERCURY CLUB

The night after the torture-chamber scene, the production trailers are back at the San Pedro docks, parked near the previous night's set. A new warehouse has been decorated to look like a Taipei nightclub. From outside, the *boom-boom* of synthesized music is muffled, the rows of windows

**Habberstad puts an arm around Isackson, while Jennifer Garner chats with Shauna Duggins, her stunt double.**

ruddy with flashing neon lights. Dozens of extras, a multi-culti mix of Asians and Euros done up in punk hairstyles and black leather bondage apparel, are making the scene at the "Mercury Club."

In the script pages for the night's shoot, the scene is set:

## INT. MERCURY CLUB—NIGHT

**MUSIC ASSAULTS US**: narcotic atmosphere—
**BODIES** writhe on the black-light **DANCE FLOOR**,
a DJ spins underground techno—
**GLIMPSES: TATTOOS, PIERCINGS**,
sex in corner shadows . . .

Sydney and Agent Vaughn are here. Garner is wearing exotic makeup and a vivid blue wig, tight black pants, and a black mesh shirt, while costume designer Laura Goldsmith has selected a long black leather jacket for Vartan. In a separate building from the main Mercury Club, the actors wait to march through what's supposed to be a bathroom of the club. As

The transformer prop "explodes" as a guard is blown into the air by the blast and Sydney Bristow races to safety.

THE LAST EPISODE

the crew gets things ready, Garner reflects on a season that's running out like the last grains of sand in an hourglass. Soon she'll be slipping into a new alias—the warrior Elektra in the feature production of *Daredevil* set to begin soon after this final episode wraps.

"It's very emotional. I have huge memories of what all our characters have been through this year," Garner says softly. "This final episode draws on how much I love everybody. It's really been great having J.J. direct, it's like coming full circle, sitting in that torture room."

At the mention of Ric Young's Suit and Glasses, her eyes go wide. "I think my stomach would drop if he walked in right now! I have fond thoughts of him as a person, but it really affects you to go through something like that [a torture scene] for days on end. I think Bradley feels the same way; I talked to him today and he was exhausted, just exhausted. Elated that he'd done it, but also exhausted by the process. I felt bad because he [Ric Young] was the only person I didn't connect with on the pilot—but he was torturing me! I think there was a natural defense built up. I never let him in, so it was easier for me to go there, and he kind of did the same thing. It was so clear from the beginning what his role meant to both of us, so we stayed away from each other. It wasn't until after we were done that I could say, 'Hi! How are you?' But Ric is a very nice man. It's like with Victor; we were so close from the beginning and we can't stand that our characters can't get along, that they have this rift."

Finally, the shot is ready and Garner joins Vartan. Outside, head makeup artist Angela Nogaro and hairstylist Michael Reitz wait among the crew and costumed extras. The makeup work is divided, Nogaro explains, so Diana Brown worked the torture room the night before because she always does Cooper's makeup, while Nogaro takes care of Garner's. It helps, she explains, to catch a day off amid those sixteen-hour days typical throughout the season.

After the transformer pyrotechnics, the energized cast and crew surrounds Video Village as DP Michael Bonvillain and J. J. Abrams (center) view a playback and exult over the result.

From left: Ben Weinert, boom operator; Ross Judd, Steadicam operator; Jeff Habberstad; Maria Bradley, wardrobe; Noga Isackson; Jennifer Garner; Shauna Duggins; Bonvillain and Abrams; Brian O'Kelley, second assistant director; Sarah Caplan, producer; Kathina Szeto, first A.C.

While Nogaro did everything from the conservative look for Garner's SD-6 persona to tonight's punked-up party girl, there were times when makeup also had to cover bumps and bruises, notably in a fight scene for "The Box" when Garner took a header into Judd's Steadicam camera. "For almost two weeks this bump on her forehead was literally green," Nogaro recalls. "We used makeup to camouflage and flatten it."

Reitz notes that hair and makeup work together. Whatever hair he'd design—from Swedish blond to tonight's "fetish club" number—was ultimately supplied by Renate Leuschner. "She's the best in town, the go-to woman," Reitz said, noting that natural-hair wigs can run to five thousand dollars apiece. "The wigs are handmade to a mold we'd made of Jennifer's head. They do the color and style we request and we get the wigs and then cut and style them. This show is excellent for both hair and makeup, and Angela and I work so well together. Like, this morning I put the blue wig on Jennifer and it was 'Oh, my God!' But with the makeup it worked!"

After the bathroom scene, action shifts to the main Mercury Club set. As the cameras get set up, stunt coordinator Jeff Habberstad hangs out with fight coordinator David Morizot. The next day, when the production goes back to the soundstages on the Disney lot, Habberstad has a stunt to rig: sending one of the unformed Taiwanese guards flying in a pyrotechnic explosion.

The world of stunts and action is peopled by tough, no-nonsense folks who literally get to play with fire. For Morizot, trained in tae kwon do as well as jujitsu and hapkido (among other styles), the controlled violence of a staged fight is a different experience, especially for martial artists accustomed to throwing—and landing—their punches. "In a stage fight you're breaking planes of vision with the camera. There's a leap from martial arts fighting to fighting for the camera because you have to throw a punch and miss—but it can be a hit from the camera's viewpoint. The camera only has one eye and not much depth of field, so we use it to our advantage for fights and stunts to make things look more exciting."

He thought of the previous night and complimented Bradley Cooper. The actor was a pleasant surprise for the veteran fight coordinator, who was one of the two masked stuntmen who kidnapped Will in episode 15, "Page 47." It'd been an iffy thing, a narrow tunnel in Griffith Park into which Cooper had to drive his Bronco while Morizot, at the wheel of the pursuing van, cut him off. "They needed to see Bradley driving, and the camera was mounted inside his car," Morizot explained. "We did a couple tests and Jeff was confident in Bradley's abilities and Bradley was gung-ho. And he was perfect, he drove in a straight line, let me do my thing. The same when we pulled him out and roughed him up a bit. Bradley takes his hits well, he's like a natural. The same with Michael Vartan. Michael says he's not a physical person, but he plays hockey—he had a good fight in 'The Box.'

"Jennifer is one of the best actresses I've ever worked with as far as fighting," Morizot added. "She's been involved with ballet and dance, and dancers can pick up a lot of martial-arts moves. But she's also a go-getter, she'll train in the technique until she gets it right. Carl, he's a powerhouse and meticulous, like his character, Dixon—a Navy SEAL type. Victor Garber is a deadly-type fighter, each move is calculated like a strategist, and he can just explode."

Meanwhile, the Mercury Club set has gotten hot with bodies and cigarettes and stage smoke. One leather-clad lass with a whip gets some help pulling on knee-high black boots while a production assistant asks the crowd to hold off smoking their cigarettes until it's time for camera. Abrams is in the midst of this controlled chaos, setting up the choreography: Sydney and Vaughn will enter, stride across the frenzied dance floor.

The explosion of the Muller device, which floods the hallways, had Sydney and Agent Vaughn running for their lives. Storyboard artist Tom O'Neill worked out the pacing and composition for the action that ended with Vaughn trapped and swept away by the rushing water.

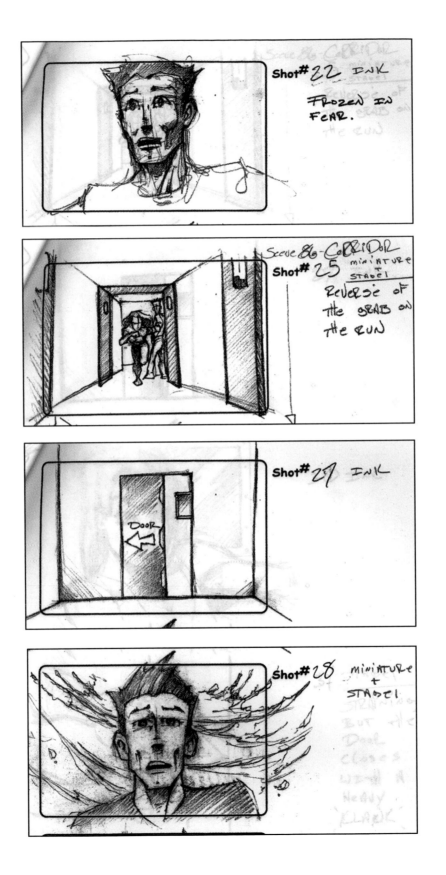

Shot#22 INK

FROZEN IN FEAR.

Scene 86 - CORRIDOR
Shot#25 MINIATURE + STAGE!

REVERSE OF THE GRAB ON THE RUN

Shot#27 INK

DOOR

Shot#28 MINIATURE + STAGE!
STRUGGLING BUT THE DOOR CLOSES WITH A HEAVY KLAKK.

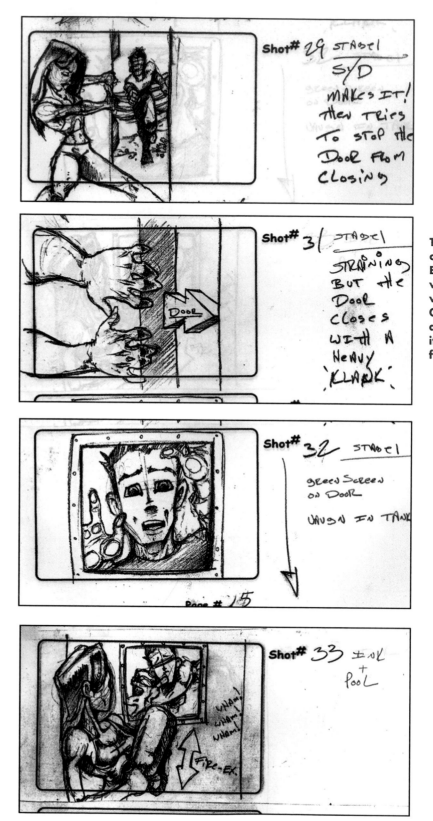

Shot# 29 STAGE 1
S/D
MAKES IT!
then tries
to stop the
Door from
Closing

Shot# 31 STAGE 1
STRAINING
BUT the
Door
Closes
WITH A
HEAVY
"KLANK"

Door

Shot# 32 STAGE 1
green screen
on Door
VAUGN IN TANK

Page # 15

Shot# 33 TANK
+
Pool

WHAM!
WHAM!
WHAM!

FIRE-EX.

These production designs worked out visual effects supervisor Kevin Blank's vision for the flood that would inundate a miniature hallway model. Footage of actors Garner and Vartan running against greenscreen was composited with the miniature hallway footage.

One dancer will grab Sydney and pull her around; Vaughn then steps back and pushes the man away, and the two agents continue on to the back of the club.

It's another Steadicam shot for Ross Judd. When Judd switches from the B camera to buckle up into his Steadicam camera rig, he looks like a superhero from a comic book, with an Iron Man–like biomechanical appendage. Judd slips on a support vest with a double-jointed spring-loaded arm connected to the Steadicam, noting the arm is loaded with titanium spring canisters. The camera itself, weighing some seventy-five pounds, balances on a three-way gimbal system, Judd explained. "It's essentially a floating camera that the operator uses, the principle being you get a more organic-feeling shot," Judd noted. "You can stay with the actors and get a smooth shot even if you're moving over rough ground. It's kind of a finger-touch feeling on the post of the Steadicam, that's what's controlling everything. I'm left-handed, so I control the Steadicam in my right hand. I come off a different side than most guys do. You hold the post as close as possible to your body without banging yourself, because the farther out you carry the weight, the more it torques your back."

The call to action is on, and Judd initially has to struggle, moving around extras who don't realize that when they're not in the shot they have to get out of the way. It's past the midnight hour as the scene comes together, but many more hours of work, other scenes, are ahead.

Behind black curtains at the back of the dance floor tonight's Video Village has been set up. It's late, but visual effects supervisor Kevin Blank is on hand, even though early in the morning he has to be in Glendale at the production's miniatures set. In an outdoor parking lot is one of the puzzle pieces of the season's biggest, most ambitious effects sequences, a fitting finale—and another example of things coming full circle.

# FIREBALL

After the hellish intimacy of the torture room and the nightclub's techno-frenzy, the third day in this stretch of filming is time for good old "movie magic" as the pieces of the season's most complex visual effects sequence are put together. It's late afternoon and the call at Stage 1 at Disney is still hours away. A short hop from Burbank—down the freeway to a Glendale exit to the gated complex of Barwick Studios, abutting the Los Angeles River—is a parking lot where Kevin Blank surveys a mass of pipe scaffolding and wood that's topped, thirty feet up, by a two-thousand-gallon water tank.

John Downey and two crew members are climbing over the structure. The special effects coordinator notes that since he can't be in two places at once, his colleague Bruce Kuroyama will supervise the other piece of the puzzle, a fireball explosion to be staged that night at the Disney soundstage.

Blank shares a copy of storyboards for the sequence marked "One Huge Ball III: VFX storyboards 'Almost Thirty Years' " (the episode's title coincidental to Jennifer Garner's thirtieth birthday on April 17). The sequence marks a full circle from the pilot, when the mysterious Muller device, created by a "modern-day alchemist," was swiped by Sydney from an FTL front in Taiwan. That unexplained device, looking like a piece of iron with a baseball-sized red ball hovering above in an anti-gravity field, was small enough for Sydney to cradle under her arm as she broke out of a secret FTL lab, her guns blazing.

Now, underneath the Mercury Club, she and Agent Vaughn discover a Muller device that's the size of a football field. Blank flips through the storyboards and outlines the sequence: The night's Stage 1 shoot includes Sydney being chased through a dark lab by Taiwanese guards until she reaches a hangar-sized "device room," where she'll discover the horse-shoe-shaped device with its massive red ball floating in the center. Sydney, one step ahead of the guards, will slap an explosive device on a power generator. In the pilot the small, hovering red ball liquefied before Sydney swiped the device, but when the generator explodes in this episode, the gargantuan red ball will cause a virtual flash flood that threatens Sydney and Vaughn as they make a desperate run down a hallway.

Downey clamps down his welding mask and goes back to work, getting the structure ready for the twenty-five-foot long scale miniature hallway model that'll be fitted onto a diagonal section of steel decking, a solid foundation that'll keep the miniature from shaking when the water is released to flood the hallway and ultimately flows out to the sloping parking lot to drain into the river. On the other side of the scaffolding, a forty-foot ground-level length of steel decking will contain miniatures of the Muller device and device room for a master shot of the initial explosion and liquefying effect.

Model makers Jim Towler and Louis Zutavern arrive to inspect the steel decking that will hold the miniatures to be delivered the next day and filmed that night. They've been working on it with famed model builder Greg Jein, whose work includes the mother ship from *Close Encounters of the Third Kind*. The model hallway's "T-section" configuration will cause the rushing water to violently ricochet around the corner at the top of the T—that was how it was done when Downey worked on *Titanic*, Blank explains.

Clearly, this is a pull-out-all-the-stops effects shot.

The miniature hallway shoot was "close to a disaster," Blank reflected. He estimated that time constraints forced his crew to accomplish four days' worth of photography in a single night. Without the time to test, they were also taking a huge risk, having only one chance to get the shot.

"We conceived the idea two weeks ago." Blank smiles. "It'd take three months to do a shot like this for a movie—we'll basically be testing this on film. We'll have one night to shoot the water. We'll shoot at night so we can control the light and use a Photosonic camera filming at two hundred forty frames per second."

Hours later, at Disney's Stage 1, the shots leading up to the generator explosion—the chase through the lab, Sydney's sprint to plant the explosive device—have been filmed and the corresponding storyboard panels, the pages of which are pinned to a bulletin board, crossed out in red. Jennifer Garner, in her blue hair and black pants, has walked forward to stare at a giant, raised sheet of greenscreen. She murmurs in awe: "Vaughn? It's bigger than I thought. . . ."

That awesome image of the football field–sized Muller device would be added later by Bob Lloyd as a 3-D computer-generated image. But the key shot that precipitates all the miniatures and digital work is a live, pyrotechnic effect of the generator exploding, and that has yet to be filmed. It's only one panel on a storyboard page, but it involves endless logistics.

Many hours before, Jeff Habberstad's crew secured to the stage floor the ratchet rig, a pneumatic cylinder for controlling airflow. It would allow a cable strung from the soundstage ceiling to yank a stuntman guard through the air, simulating the force of the explosion. Late in the evening, in a side area of the stage, Bruce Kuroyama tests the pyrotechnics. The test is serious business, requiring a fire-safety officer on hand, earplugs to shield against the big bang, and a safety perimeter behind which nonessential crew must stand.

The generator set piece itself sits at a corner of the stage in an area dressed out with stacks of crates. But it's not lit, nor are the cameras trained on it. It's getting near midnight, and rumors are floating around as to when "the explosion" will happen. For Abrams, methodically banging out shots and crossing off storyboard panels, it's as if he's saving the best for last.

"I love visual effects and movies that use visual effects in interesting ways," Abrams reflected earlier in the evening. "As a kid, I'd read effects magazines and I even approached some of the great effects people and actually developed relationships with some of them. I spent so much time taking firecrackers and blowing up models and filming them. The filming was the part that made me feel I wasn't some kind of psychopath. There was a purpose—how would it look to see this image projected? I also loved magic as a kid, and still do. That's a common theme among filmmakers, that when they were very young they loved magic and special effects. So when I approach something like this shot, it's a dream for me because I have an idea of the pieces of the sequence and how they should go together and how, when each piece is done, it'll be part of something much bigger."

As the wait goes on for the big shot, *Alias* composer Michael Giacchino, making a rare visit to the shooting set, wonders if he'll make it to the anticipated explosion since he has matinee movie plans for his kids the next day. "It's funny, the longer you're in here the smaller it seems to get," Giacchino says, surveying the soundstage, recalling how, years ago, he worked as an assistant in the Disney publicity department and often explored these soundstages, getting up into the rafters and the vertiginous catwalks.

It's after one o'clock, and the word is "Get ready." While Chris Hayes is on the main camera, Ross Judd is going to get a Steadicam angle. Garner gives Judd a hug and smiles, describing how they "dance" together—she taking the lead while Judd, the moving camera, follows.

"I'm ready to go, been ready to go," Jeff Habberstad notes of the stunt side of the shot. Meanwhile, Bruce Kuroyama works on the final touches, the pyrotechnic material ready to be triggered at the base of the generator set.

Finally, at nearly three in the morning, it's zero hour. The crew comes over to hear Habberstad explain exactly what will happen. Lean and tanned, he looks like he just got off a trail drive with John Wayne, and is as laconic as the Duke as he runs through what will happen. The bags of

The night of the shoot, several thousand gallons of water were released into the model—and the force blew the roof off the model, doused the lights, and even dented the steel decking holding the miniature. Mercifully, they'd gotten enough dramatic footage, although Blank had to digitally stabilize the hallway film because the set had buckled under impact, and also had to "up-res" the image from 6 to 100 megabytes for the detail he desired.

Although Sydney escaped through a closing door in time, Vaughn got caught. These O'Neill storyboard panels break down the close-up as Vaughn paused helplessly at the door before being swept away. The image was created in a private pool near the Disney lot, with a prop door laid over the water's surface, Vartan positioned underwater, and a camera shooting down at the actor's face, pressed against the door's window.

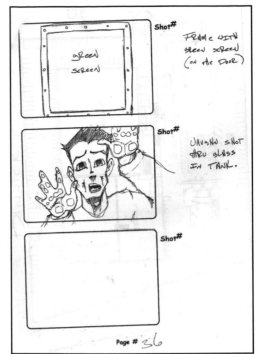

earplugs are passed around again, everyone not essential to the shot is urged back, and John Koyana, the Taiwanese guard stuntman, is given gel for the back of his head as protection from the fireball's heat. Ross Judd locks himself into his mighty Steadicam suit and Chris Hayes and Abrams discuss the angle of Garner's sprint toward the camera.

The lights are focused on the generator. Koyana is wired up. Garner toes her mark, ready to push off like a track star seconds before the explosion. After a couple of rehearsals, Abrams makes a final check before hustling back to Video Village on the other end of the stage. On the way he hands a small video camera to Giacchino, who already has a digital camera ready to document the shot. Giacchino nods. "I can handle both."

"You're awesome." Abrams salutes, heading to the monitors.

"Here we go." Giacchino smiles, juggling the cameras and taking a position behind a waist-high stack of gear in the middle of the soundstage. The set is quiet. Here it comes. . . . "Action!"

Garner, who's been running wind sprints all night, nearly slips, but that adds to the urgency. Her balance is instantly back and her legs pump as she charges toward the main camera and the guard moves after her—and the fireball blast of flame and smoke explodes from the base of the generator. The cable yanks Koyana into the air.

The dust barely settles before a crowd forms around Abrams's chair at Video Village. Jennifer Garner, Michael Vartan, and Sarah Caplan are there. Habberstad has a grin on his face, Judd is leaning close, Koyana gets a "well done" pat on the back. More production staff and crew crowd around and the circle expands. "That is fantastic!" Abrams exclaims, watching the slo-mo replay as Sydney sprints, the generator explodes, and the Taiwanese guard goes flying.

...AND SO IT ENDS...

# AND SO IT ENDS

In the season's final scene, Sydney sits in the torture room, face to face with Alexander Khasinau, who says she can now talk to his boss—The Man.

In a copy of the final *Alias* script the last lines begin with a woman's off-screen voice:

I've been waiting almost thirty years for this.

. . . and all Sydney can muster, tears in her eyes, is . . .

SYDNEY

## . . . MOM . . . ?

CUT TO BLACK.

## END SEASON ONE

"The second season we'll see much more of the family metaphor," explains writer Roberto Orci. "You'll essentially have Sydney between two parents who might or might not hate each other. That becomes the metaphor of a divorced family in which one parent betrayed the other. This is about a family that's screwed up—they just happen to be spies. That's the disguise; this is about a dysfunctional family."

It's the moment Garner told *Entertainment Weekly* she'd been waiting to learn all season. Except . . . Garner admitted she actually knew how the season would end. Jennifer—you pulled a Sydney Bristow move! "I just had to lie," she laughed, "because if he [the writer] knew that I knew I wouldn't be able to keep from telling him."

It was tough, in the Internet age, to keep a lid on all the season's surprises. "Someone, somehow, managed to leak some of the scripts onto the Internet," Scott Chambliss revealed, "sometimes as quickly as four hours after the scripts had been distributed!"

A mole within *Alias*?

"It's totally fitting," Chambliss said, laughing, "and, to me, a great publicity angle. But nobody else thought so!"

By the last week of April 2002, with production wrapping and the summer break ahead, such worries were over for a few blissful months. For cast and crew it had been a long journey through the fog of the season to reach that mountain that had been in J. J. Abrams's sights from the start. Indeed, there was a summer-vacation feeling around the production offices that final wrap week. Victor Garber seemed to personify the spirit as he strode across the lot the last Friday of the season. It was sunny, there was a breeze in the air, and he didn't seem to have a care, walking tall—a startling contrast to the world-weary figure of Jack Bristow. It was time to remove, for a while, the mask of Jack. "Time to go home, back to New York," Garber said with a bright smile.

"At the start of the season things are exciting," Michael Bonvillain noted. "But there's a rhythm to episodic television—it's a marathon, not a sprint. Things get hard, then it gets easy. Then Christmas is coming, and sud-

denly there are two episodes to go and people are getting wistful: 'What are you going to be doing this summer?'"

Soon enough, Abrams would rev up the engine and head for a new, distant mountain, brainstorming all the way. The writers would begin plotting in the writers' room, erecting the tent poles of a new season, filling that bulletin board with plot points.

"I've gotten more recognition from this show than anything I've done in my life," Ron Rifkin says with pleasure. "People walk by and yell, 'SD-6!' We were all in Las Vegas and these young women grabbed me and Victor and started yelling and screaming, 'It's our favorite show!' If it was Bradley, we could understand, but it was us, the two older guys! It was very funny."

**"I think the joy of this show for people watching has to do with the joy people have making it,"** says Ken Olin. **"That's really a testament to the environment J.J. creates and that Jennifer sets up. I don't think Jennifer appreciates how impossible this show would be without her."**

All of the cast were intrigued about the possibilities of their characters for the season to come. Kevin Weisman was hopeful that Marshall would get to go on some missions. Carl Lumbly wanted to learn the truth about Sydney and SD-6, to return to that brief time in the pilot before Sydney became a double agent, when Dixon and Sydney were truly "partners in a shared cause. I'd also like to think that we can shake up Sloane," Lumbly added with a grin.

"I think she had such a rough time this year—I'm really looking for some levity for her the next season," Garner said of her character. "But there's not one relationship I'm not intrigued by. I can't wait to see what comes up next."

If there was another wish among the actors, it was that their bond would remain unbroken. Michael Vartan, musing on the nature of their camaraderie, offered that maybe it was because they'd all been around and knew a good thing when they saw it. "There have been times when I've been driving and I'll look up and there's the Hollywood sign and I'll think, 'Wow, I made it, I'm a working actor in Hollywood!'" Vartan said. "How many people have come to this town with that dream and gone home brokenhearted? I don't know how long it'll last for me, but so far, so good. But I always swore to myself that no matter what happened on this path I've chosen, I'd never take things too seriously. At the end of the day it's fun, a great escape—it's all about make-believe."

And that may be the secret at the heart of *Alias*. It's that joy of creation, that childhood love of magic that sticks even into adulthood. Maybe the final image that sums things up is that creative circle around J.J. as they all watched the replay of the generator explosion. The assembled cast and crew had been working all night, dawn was only a few hours away, but a fantastic dream image had been brainstormed, scripted, drawn on paper—and they'd just made it real.

The moving image of secret agent Sydney escaping the explosion was cut into the final show and broadcast to the nation. Those invisible broadcast waves then radiated to the sky and into the infinity of outer space. For Abrams, who once filmed Super 8's of firecrackers blowing up models, that might be the greatest magic trick this side of forever: pure imagination made spirit.

# ACKNOWLEDGMENTS

Thanks to Wendy Loggia at Random House for her unflagging high spirits and expert editorial guidance; Kenny Holcomb for a bang-up design job; head honcho Beverly Horowitz; copy queens Colleen Fellingham, Jennifer L. Black, and Barbara Perris; marketing whiz Diane Cain; online guru Mary Beth Kilkelly; publicist Kathy Dunn; and Matthew P. Ettinger, Rebccca Price, Janet Parker, and Raina Putter for making it work—and here's a shout out to editor Steve Saffel for recommending me for this mission. Here's a salute to ABC's Bruce Gersh, who helped keep the Big Picture in focus. Bruce's assistant, Melissa Harling, was a marvel, deftly and swiftly handling everything from interview requests to background info. And a big thank-you to Chris Call for gathering terrific prop shots, photo guru Adam Larkey, and the folks who run the *Alias* Web site.

The production, led by J. J. Abrams, was gracious and welcoming—a special appreciation to J.J.'s assistant, Marybeth Sprows. Inimitable co-producer Tiffany Rocquémore-Delorme helped make straight the way through the world of *Alias*, and her assistant, Grace Kwon, was another marvel who helped with logistics and fact-checking. A tip of the hat to Rudy Gaborno (may you get that writing gig) and Nicole King, Jennifer Garner's publicist. A low bow to all cast and crew, who graciously gave of their time and insights.

Finally, thanks to my father, a huge *Alias* fan, and my mother, ever the comforting resource . . . My fond appreciation to my agent, Victoria Shoemaker . . . Here's a "Howdy" to Howard Green . . . Another shout out to Terry Jones, another huge *Alias* fan (TJ, I "got" it). And here's hoping that somewhere in this wide, wonderful world Sydney Bristow catches a little peace.

## ALIAS CREW LIST

J. J. Abrams, Creator/Executive Producer; Marybeth Sprows, Assistant to J. J. Abrams; John Eisendrath, Executive Producer; Ken Olin, Executive Producer; Linda "Sparky" Hawes, Assistant to Ken Olin; Sarah Caplan, Producer; Meighan Offield, Assistant to Sarah Caplan; Alex Kurtzman, Supervising Producer; Roberto Orci, Supervising Producer; Jesse Alexander, Producer; Jeff Pinkner, Producer; Vanessa Taylor, Co-Producer; Daniel Arkin, Co-Producer; Tiffany Rocquémore-Delorme, Co-Producer; Grace Kwon, Assistant to Tiffany Rocquémore-Delorme; Debra Fisher, Staff Writer; Erica Messer, Staff Writer; Sean Gerace, Writer's Assistant; Kelly Dennis, Writer's Assistant; Wendy Mericle, Script Coordinator; Rick Orci, Technical Consultant

## PRODUCTION OFFICE

Bob Williams, Unit Production Manager; Rex Camphuis, Production Coordinator; Michelle Guyton, Assistant Production Coordinator; Kathlene Samick, Production Secretary; Rudy Gaborno, Production Assistant; Danny Rodriquez, Production Assistant; Jef Newby, Intern; Juliana Janes, Assistant to Jennifer Garner

## ACCOUNTING

Vince Robinette, Production Accountant; James Aveler, 1st Assistant Accountant; Kevin Rogers, 2nd Assistant Accountant; Mark Kurzweil, Accounting Clerk; Mike Dewitt, Finance Production Assistant

## ASSISTANT DIRECTORS

Suzanne Geiger, Assistant Unit Production Manager; Richard Coad, 1st Assistant Director; Noga Isackson, 1st Assistant Director; Brian O'Kelley, 2nd Assistant Director; Juana Franklin, 2nd 2nd Assistant Director; Laurie Baron, DGA Trainee; John Tagamolia, DGA Trainee; Stacy Schrader, DGA Trainee; Vernon Davidson, DGA Trainee; Danny Bress, Set Production Assistant

## ART DEPARTMENT

Scott Chambliss, Production Designer; Cecele De Stefano, Art Director; Glenn Rivers, Set Designer; Brian Ellison, Art Department Coordinator; Doug Blair, Art Department Production Assistant

## CAMERA

Michael Bonvillain, Director of Photography; Tom Yatsko, 2nd Unit Director of Photography; Chris Hayes, Camera Operator; Kathina Szeto, 1st Assistant Camera; Jim Jost, 2nd Assistant Camera; Dale R. Vance Jr., Camera Loader; Ross Judd, Steadicam Operator; Jorge Sanchez, 1st Assistant Camera—B Camera; David "Clean" Berryman, 2nd Assistant Camera—B Camera

## CASTING

April Webster, Casting Director; Mandy Sherman, Casting Associate; Pam Sherman, Casting Assistant; Chad Darnell, Extras Casting—Central Casting; Summer Wesson, Extras Casting—Central Casting

## CATERING

Antonio De Leon, A & M Catering

## CONSTRUCTION

Johnny Knight, Construction Coordinator;  Jefferson Murff, Construction Foreman; John Kaiser, Lanny Henson, Tom Ivanjack, Dan Beebe, Dee Edward Phillips, Dennis Richardson, Don Silva, JP Bittl, Jerry Miller, John Empero, Justin Doran, Keith Tarello, Victor Shannon, John Borgese

## CRAFT SERVICE

Jim Smith, Ramon Galvez

## EDITORIAL

Mary Jo Markey, Editor; Ginny Katz, Editor; Maryann Brandon, Editor; Imelda Betiong, Assistant Editor; Kristin Windell, Assistant Editor

## ELECTRIC

John Smith, Gaffer; Peter Smith, Best Boy Electric; Jay Laws, Eric West, Justin Strogh, Billy Little, John Pierce, Mike Schuyler, Mike Hennesey, Clint Acquistapace

## FIRST AID

Tony Penido, Medic

## GRIP

Duanne Journey, Key Grip; Chris Godfrey, Best Boy Grip; Edmundo Sepulveda, Jeff Journey, Jason Talbert, Titus Mischke, Ellis James

## HAIR AND MAKEUP

Angela Nogara, Head Makeup; Diana Brown, Assistant Makeup; Michael Reitz, Head Hairstylist; Karen Bartek, Assistant Hair

## LOCATIONS

Mike Haro, Location Manager; Becky Brake, Location Manager; Jennifer King, Assistant Locations; Laura Lee Kasten, Assistant Locations; Pedro Mata, Assistant Locations

## MUSIC

Michael Giacchino, Composer; Madonna Wade-Reed, Music Supervisor; Jennifer Pyken, Music Supervisor

## POST-PRODUCTION

Chad Savage, Producer; Nicole Carrasco, Associate Producer; Bryan Burk, Associate Producer; Scott Collins, Post-Production Supervisor; Steve Judge, Post-Production Assistant

## PROPERTY

Christopher Call, Property Master; Christopher Redmond, Assistant Property Master; Sarah Bullion, Prop Assistant; China Iwata, Prop Assistant

## SCRIPT SUPERVISOR

Tricia Goken, Script Supervisor; Harri James, 2nd Unit Script Supervisor

## SET DRESSING

Karen Manthey, Set Decorator; Craig Gadsby, William De Biasio, Kris Fuller, Phillip Thoman, Eric Olsen, Perry Diaz, Alex Walker, Michael Magno, Paul Ilsley

## SOUND

Doug Axtell, Production Sound Mixer; Ben Weinert, Boom Operator; Javier Hernandez, Cable Person; Jeffrey Humphreys, Cable Person

## SPECIAL EFFECTS

John Downey, Special Effects Coordinator; Douglass Ziegler, Special Effects Technician

## STORYBOARDS

Tom O'Neill, Conceptualist

## STUNTS

Jeff Habberstad, Stunt Coordinator; Julia Helling, Assistant to Jeff Habberstad; David Morizot, Fight Coordinator; Jake Lombard, Stunt Safety; Merritt Yohnka, Stunt Safety; Shauna Duggins, Sydney Stunt Double

## TRANSPORTATION

Marlo Hellerstein, Transportation Coordinator; Rick Kelleher, Transportation Captain; Daron Bojarksi, Kelly Aldrich, Leanne Placek, Ed Shekter, Glenn Piccininno, John Gawrich, John Morello, William Reinhert

## VIDEO

Richard Clark, Inter Video; Dean Striepeke, Mike Ottevanger

## VISUAL EFFECTS

Kevin Blank, Visual Effects Supervisor

## WARDROBE

Laura Goldsmith, Costume Designer; Kiki Garwood, Costume Supervisor; Wendy Greiner, Key Costumer; John Doyle, Set Costumer; Maria Bradley, Set Costumer; Megan Shaw, Wardrobe Production Assistant

# ADDITIONAL CREW FROM PILOT EPISODE

Robyn-Alain Feldman, Associate Producer

## PRODUCTION OFFICE

Dan Penhale, Assistant Production Coordinator; Sharon Eldridge, Script Coordinator; Chris Cragnotti, Production Assistant; Michael Murphree, Production Assistant; Bob Lezak, Stage Manager

## ACCOUNTING

Joan Goldberg-Munch, First Production Accountant; Vicki Beck, Assistant Accoutant; Martin Tease, Accounting PA

## ASSISTANT DIRECTORS

Jeffrey Ellis, 1st Assistant Director; Rose Unite, 2nd 2nd Assistant Director; Tyrone Walker, Additional 2nd Assistant Director

## ART DEPARTMENT

Nicole Koenigsberger, Set Designer

## CAMERA

Joshua Blakeslee, 2nd Assistant Camera; David Garden, Loader; John Vetter, Loader

## CASTING

Megan McConnell, Casting Director; Janet Gilmore, Casting Director; Jonell Dunn, Casting Associate; Jennifer Lare, Casting Assistant

## CONSTRUCTION

Stephen Gindorf, Construction Foreman; John Passanante, Paint Foreman

## CRAFT SERVICE

Judy Dale Torres

## EDITORIAL

Stan Salfas, Editor; Quincy Gunderson, Assistant Editor

## ELECTRIC

Marshall Adams, Gaffer; Andrew Smith, Best Boy Electric; Steve Cooke, Mark Hartman, Brian Webster

## GRIP

Robert Ivanjack, Charles Simons, Peter Wessel, Max Gerson

## HAIR AND MAKEUP

Susan Kelber, Head Hairstylist

## LOCATIONS

Brad Bemis, Location Manager; Jennifer Lung, Key Assistant Location Manager; Michelle Heyman, Assistant Location Manager; Thomas "Bud" Blackburn Jr., Locations Production Assistant

## POST-PRODUCTION

Jon Petrovich, Post-Production Coordinator

## PROPERTY

David Scott, Property Master; Alisha Rothman, Assistant Prop Master; Stu Watnick, Assistant Prop Master

## SET DRESSING

Christopher Kennedy, Chris Webb, Rosie Tupta, Michael Vojvoda, Joel Osborne, Peter Lakoff

## SOUND

Bo Harwood, Sound Mixer; Mark Jennings, Boom Operator; Laura Rush, Cable Person

## SPECIAL EFFECTS

Tom Fisher, Special Effects Supervisor

## STUNTS

Ron Stein, Stunt Coordinator; John P. Medlen, Fight Coordinator

## TRANSPORTATION

Steve deLeon, Transportation Coordinator; Steve Garcia, Transportation Captain Visual Effects;

## VISUAL EFFECT SUPERVISOR

Alan Munro

## WARDROBE

Linda Serijan-Fasmer, Costume Designer; Anne Hartley, Key Costumer; Erik Spangler, Additional Costumer; Josephine Willes, Additional Costumer; Behnaz Shokouhi, Additional Costumer

**MARK COTTA VAZ** has written fourteen books. In addition to stepping into the world of **ALIAS**, he's explored the *Star Wars* universe (*The Art of Star Wars Episode II*) and profiled Batman and Spider-Man (*Tales of the Dark Knight* and *Behind the Mask of Spider-Man*). He's authored, with Craig Barron, *The Invisible Art*, the first major work on the legends and history of movie matte painting. He's currently at work on a history of two of the most distinguished segregated units of World War II.